LESSER HUNGERS

Rien Gray

SLASHIC HORROR
PRESS

ISBN-13: 978-1-7637256-3-8

Edited by David-Jack Fletcher.

Interior Design by David-Jack Fletcher.

Cover Design by Christy Aldridge of Grim Poppy Designs.

Content Notes

This story contains descriptions of violence, body horror, past drug use/addiction, incidents of misgendering/transphobia and police brutality.

"IT'S THE CITY ITSELF. You think of it as just a place on the map, don't you? ... There's an intelligence of its own hanging over this place... and when you breathe too much of it for too long, it gets under your skin. Then you can go anywhere – home or anywhere else – and you just keep on being what it made you from then on."

– Deadline At Dawn (1944)

ONE

I'M PROPPED UP ON the bathroom floor with a vein wide open when Nikki Gardner knocks on my door. Blood spreads across a topography of false starts and track marks, hatched red lines begging for more. Company complicates that.

Her timing is terrible. The cheap red plastic mixing-cum-ritual bowl by my wrist sits half full, but I won't be able to finish before she starts wondering where the hell I am. If she's hammering on wood at two in the morning, it must be urgent.

Oh well. Sleep wasn't on the menu tonight anyway.

I close both eyes and draw the blood back in. My circulatory system rebels at the cool injection, bulging blue along the length of my arm. Skin strains, twitches, then collapses back into its proper shape. A razor scraping bone to nerve would be kinder, but at least the wound is closed and making me fit for company.

She knocks again. "Cameron!"

Iridescent dots eat at the corner of my vision, protesting gravity when I stand up. Exsanguination is exsanguination, even if the fluid is back where it should be.

"I'm coming."

Three opened locks later, Nikki steps into view. She's usually the well-coiffed type, high top pulled fine and tight, but sweat soaks her brow, cutting through a careful mask of bronze concealer, a few stray curls covered in a bitter sheen. Anything that could leave the alderwoman of the 49th Ward shaken is bad fucking news.

"Jesus, Nikki. You okay?" I ask.

"I'm fine." Her sigh is a sharp, quick burst—steadying. "But what I just saw isn't. Did you hear the sirens?"

Cops trawl this street like clockwork, fishing for quick fines and arrests if anyone is sleeping rough, but I'd been too busy collecting blood to notice. "Sorry. I must have missed them. What happened?"

Her brow tenses. "Two people in the co-op are dead."

"Dead?" Not rare for this part of the city, but not common either. "Were they sick?"

Nikki worked herself raw making sure the city council distributed vaccines down here, including a tracing program to make sure everyone got their updated doses. Nothing's infallible, though, not when people travel in and out of Chicago every day.

"No. Not... not sick." Nikki wipes her brow, rigid with upset. "Listen, Cam. It was so awful I called the police. *Me*, calling the police."

My surprise must show, because she smiles, joyless.

"And I was a fool to do it," she says. "Three hours for them to show. Then they took one look, covered the door in yellow tape, and left. Didn't even write up a report. It's not right."

I'm no detective, but if Nikki needs a witness to keep something from slipping through the cracks, that's simple enough. "Let me get my jacket."

"Thanks." Relief sinks her shoulders an inch. "I'll buy you some coffee at 7-11. You look pale enough to scare a ghost."

Par for the course on a ritual night. I need to finish redrawing the sigils in the apartment, but the co-op is only four buildings down, so the Pollock impression can wait.

My lined Xanthous Medical jacket from work provides a nice layer of heat, distracting from the distant throb at the base of my wrist. I check the pockets—mask, cigarettes, lighter, vials, lancet—and follow Nikki out the door.

She hustles down the stairs at a clip, every step a cacophony of noise in the tight spiral of tile and iron. Wind slices us down to size as we head out onto the street, cold enough to make my teeth ache. The intersection paints oil-damp asphalt into four quivering slices, traffic lights bending back and forth against the breeze. We cross over, seeking out the fluorescent 7, where a single beatdown Chevy rests in the parking lot.

"You hungry?" Nikki asks.

I shake my head. "Coffee will do me fine."

Bill's behind the counter tonight, tapping at his phone in the camera's blind spot. He signs a quick "Hello" our way, and Nikki signs back with a practiced politician's smile. She spends a good ten minutes walking around the same three aisles, staring at chip bags and candy bars like corporate color foil is going to offer up some answers. I know a delaying tactic when I see one, so I keep quiet, occupying myself by reading the nutritional labels off trucker pills rebranded as Adderall knockoffs. Whatever Nikki saw rattled her; she can take as much time as she needs.

The total comes to two bucks with her rewards card, and we carry the thin cardboard cups out into the parking lot. She drinks deep and so do I, although ten cents of milk can't dispel the bitterness of thrice-boiled coffee grounds. I offer a cigarette and Nikki takes it, holding out for a light until flame catches against the breeze.

Except caffeine doesn't do anything for me anymore. Nicotine doesn't either, not since my blood woke up.

I say *woke up* like a one-night stand stirring in borrowed sheets, but there's only so many ways to describe snapping to consciousness in the bathtub, neck-deep in blood and frozen in place. Elizabeth Bathory style, as if she had decided to guest star as my sleep paralysis demon. I'll never forget that weight crushing my chest, watching as all that blood—not water, not even a drop, more than a single person is ever supposed to hold—soaked back into my skin over hours and hours. When it was gone, when I could finally move again, I found out no one had seen me for three days, after a bender my old addiction therapy specialist would classify as "ill-advised".

That was a year ago. Life took a turn for the weird ever since, and considering I used to work through half a blotter every night, my tolerance for weird was already pretty fucking high.

No pun intended.

"How's work been?" Nikki asks. Most of her cigarette is burned down, even though she's only taken a few drags. The wind eats at the paper, claiming its share.

"Mind your ash," I say gently. Nikki's wrist flicks, casting away gray flakes and half the ember. "And work's fine. Scrubbing the floors and hauling garbage, same as always."

Technically, my job title is Medical Waste Coordinator, but that's a nice way the forward-thinking folks at Xanthous refer to their janitorial staff: coordinators. The clinic services an even split of queer youth, HIV positive folk, the addicted, and the unhoused, since there's more overlap than not. It means the average attendee needs the same kind of resources—meds, physicals, therapy, and blood tests. The last one comes with access to clean needles, which helps in any number of ways.

I used to be a client. Maria at the front desk was kind enough to hire me when she found out I sobered up, even if she didn't know the context.

"Maybe I should get out of politics," Nikki mutters. "Get a 9-to-5."

"I work ten at night to six a.m.," I note. My weekends are Mondays and Tuesdays—too many emergencies start on Friday night and keep rolling until Sunday morning. The clinic doesn't really close. "But it's quiet. No bullshit. Nothing but my music and a big ring of keys."

She manages a smile. "I like people too much. Every time we get another park bench or open up a community garden, I know it's because I worked the city until they spit out the coin we deserve. People's lives actually change."

Nikki fixes things out in the open: getting clean water in new pipes, speed bumps in front of the school, enough places to vote for the whole neighborhood. Her work gets complicated when half our taxes land in Chicago PD's pocket, and harder still when they show up to upset our local balance. Peace is as fragile and demanding as a hothouse orchid.

So I do my best to repair what falls through the cracks. Helping kids sleeping in the outdoor stairwells get somewhere with a mattress, giving out Narcan from the clinic when it hits shelf date—the juice lasts a year longer than they're allowed to keep the boxes—or whatever else comes up. I even broke into an apartment once to get credit cards and IDs back from a lady's health-guru-turned-cultist boyfriend. He had locked everything up and tossed her out to "break the chains of society around her neck."

"Scene must be real bad if you're sipping that crude oil so slow," I say as Nikki stubs out the last of the cigarette. "Losing people isn't easy."

"The dying is bad enough, but this…" She shakes her head—a knife-like jerk, trying to cut the tension gripping her neck. "They were just kids, Cam. A happy couple. This was their first place together."

"Do I know them?"

Nikki frowns. "I don't think so. Patricia and Scott Hayes. College sweethearts. Had young, white, and successful written everywhere until she got in a bad car accident. Medical bills and Chicago State debt tore that foundation down."

Explains why they were living in the co-op. Some people choose it for the socialist bent, but most are struggling, and the promise of rent control overrides any misgivings about a communal dining room. Nikki offered me a spot there once, but even before I started splashing the inside of my veins on the walls, a primal need for privacy kept me away. Whether it was reflex to hide my laundry list of addictions or the trauma of being nonbinary in too many locker rooms, who's to say? Regardless, I've always needed my space.

"Car accidents go hand-in-hand with opiate prescriptions." After another sip of battery acid masquerading as dark roast, I chuck the still-warm cup into the trash. "You know how much can go wrong there."

"Not like this." Nikki crumples her coffee into a ball of beige-soaked cardboard before throwing it away. "Come on."

We duck back across the street and a block over to the hooked black fence surrounding the co-op. It takes four tries for Nikki's key to catch the lock before a curse and the hard twist of her wrist does the trick. The building is like a thousand others in the Chicago interior: arranged out of lumpy salmon brick molded from Lake Michigan clay, slapped together post-fire to cover the ruins of a block turned to ash. I doubt anyone expected something so cheap to last into the next century, but if we're known for anything here, it's stubbornness.

Her stairwell mirrors mine. The only difference is the long hall stretching past it, with a line of closets on one side and a reinforced glass door on the other. Outside that is a square of shared concrete where summer chairs and ashtrays jockey for position with homemade flowerbeds and a host of scrappy vegetables climbing a trellis. The garden-slash-courtyard has spent years as a poster child for human reconciliation, which is why it feels so strange to be climbing up the steps to a pair of corpses.

The second floor is dark at this hour, cast in shadows by two points of light: the mandated fluorescent above the stairs, and a dull green emergency exit sign bolted above an opposing window. Nikki abandons her keyring before pulling out a singular disconnected key from her other pocket and offering it up.

"Building's backup."

"Where did their set go?" I ask.

She swallows, hard enough to stick. "Still inside, I think."

Two doors down, I spy the crime tape. CPD did shoddy work, leaving behind a slanted *X* with yellow arms of DO NOT CROSS that would clothesline anyone trying to get through. Nikki doesn't say anything when I tug the tape out of the way, but she doesn't move to follow me either. Even if the cops ditched the scene, I'm technically still trespassing.

Not that Nikki is some kind of law and order type. Any alderwoman knows the score even better than I do, but her public-facing work could be jeopardized by association. I don't have any kind of reputation to uphold on my end.

Which is for the best. I'm no therapist or activist, any sort of change-maker. I'm not even a particularly good person. What I am is a thirty-year-old asshole that would have been rotting in the ground a decade back if this neighborhood hadn't taken care of me. If the thing sleeping under my skin helps with that, so much the better.

"I can't," she whispers as I fit the key into the lock. "I'm sorry. I can't see it again."

"How long have they been in there?"

"Dead, you mean?" When I nod, she clarifies. "A day. Less, maybe. They brought chili to the Sunday potluck. Everything seemed fine."

Out of an abundance of caution, I take my mask out and put it on. A few layers of fabric isn't a respirator, but anything helps. "You found them yourself?"

"Yeah." Nikki clears her throat. "I had dish duty last night, so I was bringing Scott's pot back to him. Patricia leaves the front unlocked, so I didn't think anything was wrong until I walked in."

Here goes nothing. "I'm going to close the door behind me, okay?"

Her nose crinkles with confusion, but she doesn't push, so I step past the threshold, shut the door, and flip the lights on.

I'm welcomed by broken teeth.

Slivers of enamel, scattered like pills across the floor. Dried saliva slathers each piece in a plasticky sheen, marking a trail to red threads of exposed root and severed nerve. No, not severed—the cut isn't so clean. A horrible show of force wrenched them free, then shattered what remained. I follow their path to the void of a woman's mouth, jaw ripped from its mooring, hanging with a pendant's weight around her neck.

Patricia's eyes are open, bulging from fear but sunken with decay, green irises dulling gray, egg yolk soft. Heavy scratches mar one cheek, curving down to the hollow where the rest of her face should be. The other side is perversely pristine, as if blood forgot to bend to gravity's will in a moment of shock. Ragged pink edges bare a ring of fleshy cavities flanking palate and tongue, still connected despite the frame of her jaw gouged and pulled free like a particularly stubborn safety seal.

Blood is a rusting, congealed crust down the front of her pale blue Chicago Sky T-shirt, but the fabric is shredded with hand-size gaps, inches of flesh scooped out in sets of five, deep enough to expose the slick film of cartilage and tendon. One hand desperately clutches at her chest to try and keep every-thing inside, paralyzed with rigor, but the other is soaked to the wrist in darkening layers of sticky red, reaching towards the other side of the room.

Which is where I find Scott, lying on his back. His head—what remains—is halfway into the bathroom, resting on putrescent yellow tile. The man's face is more holes than flesh, separated by so many punctured crescents that it takes a second to register them as bite marks. Dozens upon dozens, chewed down to the bone. It leaves Scott's teeth exposed in a permanent rictus of pain, the only sense of structure between the masticated bulb of his nose and the burst pipe of his esoph-agus. Where the rest of his throat went is an open question.

Mine, however, burns violently with acid, and taking a deep breath only infuses my senses with the stench of cold viscera and evacuated bowels. My tongue turns to iron, tarnished with the leaden warning of rot.

I've scrubbed, scraped, and scoured bodily fluids from every imaginable surface, both at work and in my own bathroom when hangovers and comedowns exacted their price from a failing liver. The Hayes aren't the first bodies I've seen, and plenty have been in far worse shape, bloated with gangrene gas or hollowed out by a nesting scavenger. When someone commits suicide in the same room as their cat, the results are a closed casket funeral.

Those didn't make me sick, or even sad. This sends me stumbling over Scott's corpse to rip off my mask and bend over the bathroom sink. I cough up sour brown sludge and slippery bile until the coffee and then some sticks in the drain, clogging in a slow, viscous spiral around gore-choked steel. He must have made it this far before dying, because a heavy trail of blood climbs the porcelain belly of the sink, smeared across the faucets and gathered by gravity at the very bottom. Some of it flakes off under my palm, where I gripped the edge without thinking.

Good thing the cops already swept this place. I just mashed my fingerprints all over a local reproduction of Caligula.

The pieces snap together in red, red unison.

Patricia and Scott ate each other alive. At least, that's sure as hell what it looks like.

Except that doesn't explain *why* or *how*, because Scott doesn't look like he could bench the bar, much less tear his girlfriend's jaw clean off. With a second, wary glance around the apartment, the familiar signs of impending poverty make themselves known; last notice bills stacked next to clipped coupons on the kitchen table, single pairs of stripped-sole shoes by the door, half a dozen empty dollar store soup cans that must have made up the Sunday chili. With guilt churning in my gut, I yank open their medicine cabinet and find Patricia's prescription for Percocet. The orange bottle is empty, label three months expired.

Good news: the temptation thrashing in my skull has nowhere to sink its hooks. Bad news: I doubt the drugs were related, because she didn't have any left.

"What the fuck happened here?" I offer to the air, hoping for a reply.

Because there's one way to confirm the truth, but I really don't want to do it.

Delaying the inevitable, I take one of the vials out of my jacket and use the edge of the lancet to scoop the biggest gummy-like clot from the sink inside. Clicking the red cap into place almost feels professional. With the vial shut, I seal the sample away into a zippered pocket on my jacket, in case I need a little extra later.

Blood tells me everything. Ever since that night, I can read the truth in a pulse, hear the holes scarring the chambers of a stranger's heart, and calculate sugar levels with a drop rubbed between my fingers. The process is exactly as disgusting as it sounds, but finding out a sixteen-year-old is foaming at the mouth because his party supplies were spiked with Fentanyl means I can tell the EMTs exactly what to dose him with. Allergies, diabetes, cancer—it's all just waiting for me to take a taste. On top of everything else, I'm a walking HIPAA violation.

So I put the blade to my tongue, curse the cosmic joke of my existence, and lick it clean. The sensation is always the same—cold and dull as a copper penny. Which is why it's kind of a surprise when I seize and hit my head so hard against the towel bar that the world kaleidoscopes.

"God*damn* it."

Sheer luck keeps me from stabbing myself through the mouth, although it wouldn't matter much. Whatever's clinging to me doesn't like being pierced through. Grabbing a used syringe the wrong way at work one day was proof enough; the needle was shoved out so fast it left me dizzy. I'm in the same state now, brain-bruised and scrounging for balance.

I didn't learn anything. It should have been like an invisible hand passing over a Post-it note of chemicals and conditions—this was a cattle prod to the tonsils. Now I don't have a clue what Patricia and Scott did to each other, but I do have a migraine. Not to mention playing taste-that-trauma on a dead man is worth at least three showers' worth of shame.

The front door jostles open.

Nikki calls out, "Cam, are you okay?"

With trembling fingers, I shove the lancet back into my jacket. "Yeah, I... I got sick. Be out in a second."

When the hinges swing shut again, I manage to stand upright. I have to ignore Scott's grisly handprints to get a good look in the mirror, but my reflection is no less ghoulish. Both eyes are shot enough to count the capillaries, pupils blown black hole wide and devouring the hazel of each iris. A line of blood slips down the side of my mouth like a B-movie vampire, so I turn both faucets on to try and wash everything off.

The cold side spins to no avail, but after a couple of choked bursts, the hot knob spits out a lukewarm stream. It tastes unfiltered, but I'll take the limestone over whatever the hell that was a minute ago. Once my face is clean, I dry off with the closest towel and step back over Scott, giving him as big a berth as I can.

A place this small only has a few windows, but both of them are closed, and by the dust, no one's cranked them open in months. Considering the state of things, a break-in seems pretty damn unlikely, but I owe it to the pair on the floor to work through the possibilities. Which means a good old-fashioned stash hunt.

The fridge, couch cushions, and TV case are easy marks, but they're empty of everything but crumbs and undefinable stains. Rifling through every cabinet with the Hayes a few feet away is inherently disrespectful, but at least I'm not one of those poor bastards that can see ghosts.

In the plural, anyway.

By the time I'm groping the wallpaper for hollow spaces behind it, the 'lost cause' bell in my head is ringing. Certain chemical mistakes are known for provoking rage, but the accompanying residue—paraphernalia, rainbow oil burns on the stove, the slow corrosion of smoke on paint—simply isn't here.

My head is already cracked, and I'd rather not bring more ruin to a place Nikki is already going to have to pay an arm and a leg to clean. So I tug my mask back on and duck into the hallway, grateful for the barrier of cotton hiding any leftover red on my teeth.

"I threw up too," Nikki says. Dark eyes sweep me over from head to toe. "Managed to make it out to the hallway, though."

"Sorry. I aimed for the sink." Shoving both hands in my jacket pockets, I grip the lancet to keep from fidgeting. Even sober, I tend to twitch. "The cops really looked at that horror show and turned right around?"

Her smile is more wince than teeth. "They said it was a domestic disturbance."

"Two people *cannibalizing* each other is a domestic disturbance? Even murder-suicides usually get the medical examiner."

"Did they actually—" Nausea pulls Nikki's face tight. "Cam, don't tell me that. Someone else must have hurt them."

"Windows are closed. No other witnesses." I shrug. "You have a camera by the front door, right? Did someone sneak in?"

"No," she says distantly. "I already checked. But people don't do that to each other out of the blue. Patricia and Scott were in bad shape, but they weren't..."

"Starving?" I suggest.

Nikki's throat jumps, but she nods. "Yeah. At least I didn't think so. And who the hell turns teeth on their spouse before asking for help? Everyone's close in this co-op, Cameron. They had to know I have connections with every food bank in the city. And the good stuff too, not just canned hot dogs and beans."

The Hayes's should have, but I know why they didn't. "Too much pride, I bet."

"What?"

"Pride. The bad kind. Like, you know, charity is supposed to be for other people instead of *us*. Blame it on elitism or misplaced martyrdom, but the results are about the same."

"Sounds like you're speaking from personal experience," Nikki says.

I fake a smile. "My mother didn't have an ounce of pride in her body."

Plenty of other people did, though, and seemed compelled to make sure that she knew their opinions on the matter at every opportunity. Lecturing a single parent is a lot easier than helping her out.

"God. None of that is worth dying for." Nikki sighs. "Now what?"

Not much left but the cold logistics. "Either of them have family? Local?"

"I tried Scott's emergency contact from the co-op agreement, but no one picked up. Patricia didn't list next of kin." She frowns.

I can practically hear the tumblers of her mind spinning, one decisive click after another. "We can get them cremated. I'll pass the plate around the building and see how much can be scrounged together."

Burial's too expensive, regardless of best intentions. "Do you want me to keep digging?"

"Yeah, I do. I know what it looks like, Cam, but that's not good enough." Nikki's shoulders straighten, tight and resolute. "I want to know why. I have to. People don't get left behind under my watch. Ever."

She means it—I'm living proof. Which is why there's only one answer to give. "Okay. Scan me a copy of that co-op agreement. Then I can trace the loose threads and see if anything shakes out."

Nikki looks like she wants to hug me, but she also knows well enough not to try. "Thank you. Need an escort home?"

I frown. "No, I want you to go to bed. You're swaying on your feet."

"If you think I'm sleeping after—"

"Hey," I interrupt softly, eyes locking with hers. "Secure your own mask first. Rule number one, right?"

Same as she told me over and over when I was crawling out of the pit I made of my life, no matter how many times I fell to the bottom. Guilt and fear make it easy to burn yourself out on other people, until there's nothing left to cling to but ash. Twelve-step programs drive me up the wall, but there's a reason making amends is so far down their list. No point in apologizing for past mistakes if you're an inch from sliding back down the ladder again.

Nikki claps a hand against my shoulder. "Can't believe you're turning that shit on me."

"'Cause it's good shit," I counter with a smile. "Go to bed, Ms. Gardner. Tasha's probably waiting up for you."

At the mention of her wife, Nikki's face softens. "Yeah. She's the only reason I've been able to hold it together today. Will you be okay alone after seeing that mess?"

I'm never alone. But I can't tell Nikki that. "Don't worry. Nothing's going to keep me up with how tired I am."

She does walk me down to the front door, but I step out onto the block by myself and make the short trip back to my apartment.

Once my jacket and shoes are off, I'm determined to take my own advice and crash out. Halfway to the nest of pillows and blankets, I remember the bowl of blood sitting out in the bathroom, and my animal groan of frustration must echo up to the fourth floor.

Fuck it. The sigils can wait until tomorrow.

TWO

Late afternoon sunshine is trying to prod me awake when I get a text from Nikki:

> Co-op cobbled together a grand for services. Cheapest I can find for two people is 1200, so I'm going to hit up the city for the rest.

Good on her. In my opinion, they should rip the last chunk out of the overtime pay those cops earned doing fuck all. I scroll past her message and see Nikki sent the co-op agreement too, which means I can start poking my nose around later and pick up CPD's slack.

After texting back some generic encouragement—I'm not try-ing to be a dick, but empathy has never been my strong suit—I strip out of last night's clothes and drag the canvas tarp from its home in the closet. My landlord might as well not exist for how little he acknowledges my presence beyond the monthly payment, but if I don't take care of the box I live in, everything else will fall apart. Staining the floor with blood is a no go, on principle alone.

The tarp itself is more old wine than beige now, Rorschach blotches of venal drip and arterial spray overlapping one another, dried past the point of consequence. Over time, I've gotten better at using smaller splits for more surface area, but efficiency doesn't change the fact that whatever's inside me gets frothing mad if I don't draw weird symbols around the apartment every so often.

If I ignore the impulse, my dreams drown in red. They drown me until I wake up staring at the wall with my skin peeling apart like pages in the center of a book, a sanguine sleepwalker. So I'd rather do a bit of experimental art than deal with that horror show on a regular basis.

Old habits die hard. I tap a good vein in the crook of my elbow without looking twice, but a needle's not required when the blood just answers.

Far as I can tell, the lines don't mean anything, or if they do, my comprehension is irrelevant. I could be writing down the secrets to Atlantis and Area 51 combined, but there's never any pattern to decrypt. Some days the paths are clear and regimented as train maps, diverting off before looping back into one another. Others demand smearing my bloody palm back and forth across the wall until every vein stops singing.

Either way, the stains don't stay for long. I'm not sure if the signs scare off whatever it's afraid of—what could something like *this* be afraid of?—or because the universe is being kind enough to make sure I get my deposit back one day. I've asked why I'm going to so much trouble, in my head and out loud, to dead silence. There's no voice, no explanation, just urges.

Maybe it chose me because giving into urges is the only thing I'm good at.

I finish, roll up the tarp, and put everything away. Staring at the sigils is bound to make my head hurt, and the crushing ache in the back of my skull from the towel bar has yet to fade. Taking pain meds is out of the question when my blood-based parole officer will turn the pills into placebos.

After a long shower, I wash the crust of last night's bowl out in the sink and put on water for coffee. It won't wake me up, but it's hot and familiar, which is enough of a creature comfort to keep me buying the good stuff at the shop by Morse Station.

Going through the world's worst juice cleanse doesn't mean my brain got rewired. Who I am is etched in muscle and nerve, compulsions filtered but too deep to shake. So I still notice when someone's selling on the corner. I still look at the bottom of a dead woman's pill bottle for leftovers. I still drink coffee, damn it, because no one else gets to make that choice for me.

Not even the consumptive *thing* that made me endure withdrawal from a decade plus of coke, ecstasy, miscellaneous benzos, and a budding heroin habit. The combo should have killed me too many ways to count, but it didn't. Instead I spent a hellish week in bed convulsing on sheets drenched with piss and puke, organs shriveling while my rabid hair-of-the-dog attempts to get high again failed, over and over. No drugs, new normal.

The mattress had to be thrown out, which set me back two hundred bucks and change. Nothing like making a fool of yourself and then having to pay double for it.

My phone beeps; the time is just after four-thirty. I scour the document Nikki sent, checking for employment references. Patricia has two listed, both apps: rideshare and delivery. Scott was apparently a mechanic. Explains how they were able to afford a car in the middle of the city—he must have done the maintenance himself. I doubt any of the above are going to pick up after hours, so a check-in might have to wait until tomorrow.

Honestly, it's impossible to tell how far I can chase this. What are the chances some app manager is going to know about Patricia's personal life? Was Scott sharing spousal squabbles with someone on the creeper seat next to him? Maybe, but I doubt it would be enough to explain what I found in the apartment.

Problem is, Nikki has always been a great judge of character. Even if the character happens to be a burned-out husk like mine. When she says they wouldn't have ever done this to each other, instinct tells me to take it as gospel. So I have to go hunting—and I will, tomorrow before my shift starts.

Because today is Tuesday: date night. My girlfriend is real particular about the hours she keeps, and I do my best not to show up looking like I got dragged crossways down Main Street. Which means shoving a protein bar—eternal savior of those who lack executive function or general culinary interest—into my mouth and putting on better clothes. 'Better' is contextual, of course. A clean white T-shirt, jeans instead of joggers, and the crushed brown leather jacket I've had so long we're probably in a common law marriage.

I should tell Katherine that. She'll think it's funny.

The path to Calvary Catholic is a long but easy walk down Clark. Local landmarks haven't changed much in ten years: corporate fast food joints, the Mexican bakery selling fresh pastries by the bag, and an always-on-sale furniture store everyone knows is a front for something else. No idea what, but there isn't a single price tag in the whole damn place.

Ward 49 is a half-gentrified Frankenstein, bleeding out the Black population with rent hikes while absorbing Mexican refugees bussed in by Republican governors. Good PR from the latter muddies the crisis of the former, since the local census hangs at a certain percentage of color. Poor white queers bump up against the newly minted lower middle class, but everyone involved has too much college debt to go anywhere else.

In the alley between a car wash and opposing tattoo shops, two guys lean against the brick and catch my eye. The shorter one, too-young face hidden by a too-long beard, holds out a cup and forces a smile. It must hurt; his gums are swollen enough to swallow his teeth. Signs of scurvy, matching our societal revival of century-old illnesses—polio, measles, a killer flu. In this new age of conspiracy, disease has fucking unionized.

"Got any change on you?"

Ransacking my pockets turns up a pair of quarters, and I hand them over without reserve. I don't have much, but I do have the privilege of a roof over my head. The only times I've slept rough are nights leaving a club at last call, too wired to remember where I lived. Even on months when rent was tight, somebody went out of their way to keep my head that last crucial inch above the waterline. Not everyone gets that luxury.

"Thanks." He shifts back against the wall, but the taller man leans in with a frown. Recognition flares across his wind-weathered face.

"You work at the clinic, don't you?"

The question reads genuine, so I relax. Every so often, people get professionally dragged out of Xanthous for threatening or assaulting staff, and carry the grudge a good long while.

"Yeah. Why?"

"Can you really walk in without an appointment?" His body stiffens, braced for the refusal. "I don't have a phone or nothin'."

"Sure can." I reach into my jacket and dig up a business card. Work hands them out like candy, encouraging us to spread the word. "Take this. Then head in and talk to Maria at the front desk. She'll get you sorted."

The card isn't strictly necessary, but I know how important it is to offer a direct invitation. Folks on the street don't get mercy or grace from almost anyone, so it's second nature to avoid places where mere proximity risks arrest—or worse.

He takes it, holding the card between two fingertips as if it's made of glass instead of paper. "Thanks. Sorry for bothering you."

"You're fine." Emotion never seems to make it to my face, so I hope tone gets the point across. "Both of you have a good day."

Okay, that might have leaned hard on the customer service voice, but I work the night shift because talking to strangers gives me hives. His head bobs in a quick nod, so I keep walking, ignoring a chain of red lights to make up some time. Almost no one drives through the one lane side streets anyway.

Clark becomes Chicago Avenue, trading rugged sidewalk for the smooth face of fresh and expensive concrete as Calvary's black fences come into view, drawing the eye to a towering white gate with Matthew 5:4 engraved across the arch. Mourning is the last thing on my mind, but the comfort happens just the same.

This place is the oldest cemetery christened by the Archdiocese of Chicago, which is to say the headstones are dominated by monumental broad-winged angels and crosses, with the occasional grave portrait scraped featureless by decades of rain and snow. No one seems to be getting buried today, so it's quiet as, well, you know. I used to come here a lot and trip, babbling at the dead and pondering the purpose of my existence. Those questions never got answered, but I did meet Katherine.

Her grave is a small brass plaque, identical to the dozens of others not rich or glorious enough to command a mausoleum. Katherine holds the dubious honor of being one of the first ones buried here, right after the Great Fire killed her and three hundred other people. After all this time, she loathes open flame more than anything else, so I keep the cigarettes buried and avoid playing with my lighter.

I urge blood to my fingertips, and bend down to slick the stone. From what Katherine tells me, even the dead who linger need a human anchor. Without the living, they're completely invisible. A hint of sacrifice—or more, if you're so inclined—will do the trick.

The air thickens with cold, and in the mirror of frost, the lines of her face come together. Everything else is a nebulous mist, thin enough to be mistaken as fog by anyone watching more than a few feet away.

"Good evening, Cameron." She smiles and moves like a coil of smoke, filtering through my lips and teeth. Not a kiss, exactly, but

I like it better. "Keep making that face, and your frown is going to be permanent."

I'm given that warning every week. "It makes me look distinguished, Kat."

Her laugh is a stolen sound, wind warped by a half-lost memory of lungs and steady breath. "Are we going for a walk tonight?"

"Yeah." This time, I do smile. "Come on in."

For a second, everything is desperately electric as a car battery starting under two feet of snow. Katherine's presence is numb heat, spreading until she settles in my skin. She tests my fingers by forming a fist, working through each limb until everything is under her control.

Possession is a word with a lot of weighted implication. This body is barely mine anyway, never recognized in the way I need it to be. I could stitch every inch of skin with patches and pins declaring THEY and THEM, and some smirking bastard on the street would still ask if I'm "One of those he-shes from the drag show on Netflix." What's the point?

Handing over the keys is a relief. Katherine gets the privilege of flesh and bone again, and I don't have to drive. My body isn't anything like the one she used to have, but she insists the differences don't bother her. Nothing about me bothers her, which begs the question how I got so damn lucky.

"Lakeside and back?" she asks, although it's my voice on exit.

"Sounds good to me."

One downside of us hooking up is that it looks like I'm talking to myself, but I've gotten stares for less. We leave the cemetery out the back path and make a beeline for open water, slow and measured. Katherine's pace quickens as she remembers the mechanics, slipping her hands into my pockets. They convulse, curling in like claws.

"What has you so tense?" She withdraws just enough to seize my shoulders in a morgue-cold grip, pulling them down and back into alignment. "That chisler you were telling me about a while ago? Tommy?"

The name conjures up a dim and angry haze, which doesn't help much. A lot of names do that, and my memory is a sieve on the best of days. "No?"

She dismisses the question with a sigh. "Just tell me what happened, honey."

I relay what happened at the co-op, sparing no detail. Maybe some 19th century women would be scandalized by such things, but Katherine was a Gold Rush export to the Midwest brewing whiskey under watchful Irish eyes, and half their stock went to laudanum dens. Add in a hundred and fifty years as a spectral citizen, and she's seen pretty much everything.

"Ever heard of people dying like that before?" I ask.

"No." Katherine frowns, pulling my brow down tight. "I mean, people lost in the middle of nowhere and doing the desperate thing, sure. And that Boone Helm fellow back in the day. But I think he just liked killing, and the eating was happenstance."

Nothing like a married couple who showed up to the potluck one night and tore each other apart the next. "Me either. Nikki wants me to look into it, though."

"She's a sharp woman," Katherine says. Hearing such warmth in my voice is always inescapably strange. "Something like that wouldn't sit right with me either."

"I know. Except the only lead I have is looking into their jobs. And I don't really think a co-worker is going to tell me why Patricia rearranged Scott's face into an appetizer."

"Either of them troubled in the head?" she asks.

"Not that Nikki mentioned."

Then again, she might not know. We like to think that if someone close to us is hurting, we would be the first to figure it out, but that's rarely true. I spent every morning getting high for months on end before someone ever asked to my face if anything was wrong. No one would define me as a so-called 'functional' addict either. At the end of the day, most people worry that acknowledging the truth obliges them to do something about it, and acting like everything is on the level feels easier.

Hell, I've done the same. One of my old rave buddies had a two-bag-a-day meth habit, and I always asked how he was doing, even though he had less teeth each time we hung out. After he OD'd one night and died, everyone had the gall to act surprised, even his dealer. His funeral was beset by a fog of *I should have said something*, but when we're all guilty, who bothers to take the blame?

Katherine and I walk down the narrow concrete pier that stretches out into Lake Michigan, divided twice over by a barrier in the center. Why they strung hard black wire through half-bent steel pikes and made it even easier to fall off, I can't say. The wind picks up as we reach the end, stopping where a short red lighthouse offers a ladder ten feet high.

The steel rungs are tall enough to hang from, but not much else. A spinning light at the top keeps the occasional weekender with a ten-footer from accidentally running aground, sure, but anything big enough to need the warning from a distance wouldn't be able to see past gray waves and the creeping light of the skyline.

She sits on the cool concrete edge, letting my work boots hang a few inches above the water. "Did you try the blood?"

Katherine is the single person in my life who knows about the rituals. They're the only reason I can see her at all, and by any measure, that's unusual enough. In decades, she's only met two other people who could sense a ghost, but they were plagued by seeing every kind of dead, and Katherine never found any connection between them. One made bank running séance scams until she was driven out of the city, and the other shot himself after too many tragic spirits tried to climb through him like a fire escape.

Nothing with my definition. Half the time I wonder if I'm simply sick, if this is some illness science hasn't caught onto yet—porphyria redux, or the next evolution of prion disease warping my blood into something it shouldn't be.

I guess it doesn't matter. My body betrayed me a thousand times growing up, so what's one more? At least I have Kat.

"Of course," I answer. "Felt like putting my tongue in an electric socket."

Her confusion wrinkles my nose. "Funny. Did you just try the once?"

"Yeah, since the first time made me clock my head into the wall."

"That's what the soft spot's from," she mutters, reaching back to brush tender fingers through my hair. "Best be careful. You don't have enough white matter in there to begin with."

I laugh. "Thanks, babe."

"You know what I meant," Katherine huffs. My hand drops back down, knuckles resting against the pier. "I plan on keeping you around a good long time, Cameron Ciris. And I take poorly to disappointment."

Which makes it even more shocking that she's dating me. I've never had to explain our relationship to anyone before, but even if I did, I imagine the average bystander would assume my end of the deal leans raw. What do you get from a woman who isn't really here?

Acceptance, it turns out. From the first time Katherine's mist-heavy eyes took on a diamond glint, and she whispered, "You're queer like me, ain't you?", love brought me low. We're cut from different stripes, but I enjoy listening to her stories about bars and secret societies that burned down before I was even born, knowing the words I have now grew from the ruins. She learns from me in retrospect, clinging to a present she was never meant to see.

"It's not like I'd really go anywhere," I joke. "You didn't."

"Most people don't become ghosts, darling," she says, soft with warning. "So don't take that gamble on my account."

"I won't. Having you inside me is way better."

Katherine's low, scandalized laugh pulls at my heart like a glove made of black velvet. "Incorrigible soul. I wish you'd been around with me in the old days. We would have given the priests a hundred new sermons."

Oh, absolutely.

We stay on the pier a while longer, talking about nothing of consequence until the last drop of light drains out of the sky. Katherine chastises me about missing lunch, so I pick up a double order from Byron's and eat it down to the crumbs. Once she's satisfied, I leave her back at the grave and make the long walk home.

THREE

A SERPENT OF BLOOD stains yellow tile, drying to scales of rust at my feet.

The man in the bathroom is wearing a gaudy silk shirt stamped with golden crosses, spread wide open to bare his stomach. Pale and swollen, piscine. Knees spread wide enough to rouse a riot on the CTA, were he still drawing breath. Except his throat is shredded to the spine, a void of flesh curving in on itself like an open mouth.

Dead blue eyes stare at the ceiling, but looming over him, it's impossible to shake that he's glaring at me. I kneel down for a closer look, following the waterfall of blood down to his clavicles until I find what I need. A shy corner of clear plastic pokes out of the man's open trachea, and I seize it between my fingernails before slowly drawing the rest of the prize free.

The bag is crimson slick, sealed tight around smooth white seeds of ecstasy and MDMA: a candy flipper's wet dream. I set it on the tile and go in for the rest of the bounty, pushing my fingers past tight rings of cartilage and muscle rigid with rigor. Nearly lost to the knuckle, I seize another bag, just as promising.

This one falls heavy, a wet slap on tile, but I know there's more. I have to find a good grip on the man's hair and pull back hard, giving my fingers room to dowse for more.

Everything reeks of alkaline, piss washed away by impotent bleach, neither strong enough to cover the scent of fish-like decay. That doesn't stop me from digging deeper, working down to the elbow to retrieve the grand prize at the bottom of his stomach: a bag big enough to swell the organ, blooming up to the lungs.

Thick rubber bands of digestive muscle convulse around my arm, squeezing so hard flesh numbs to static as he utters, "You always were a bastard, Cameron."

Plenty of mornings start bad, but being ripped back to consciousness in a cold and sour sweat doesn't get better with exposure. The blankets are a damp tangle, clinging to my skin like moss. Lucid dreams were fun when I got high; lucid nightmares feel like divine punishment for trying to get a full eight hours of sleep.

Guess seeing the Hayes's turned to hamburger did a bigger number on me than I thought.

Dazed, I palm my phone off the bedside table and check the time. One in the afternoon—bright and early. I kick off the snarl of sheets and roll out of bed, biting back a hiss of annoyance at the hard chill of the floor. Wood cleans much easier than carpet, but unless you keep your apartment at eighty degrees, it's like walking on an ice rink.

A scorching hot shower melts away the remains of the dream, echoes of shining pills and open flesh pulling at the margins of my vision. After rounding up some scratch paper and a pen, I do another quick scan of the Hayes's co-op agreement and write down the relevant phone numbers. FastFeast is first on the list, so I dial up their customer service while brewing a fresh pot of coffee.

They keep me on hold so long I'm three-quarters through my second cup and a protein bar before the muffled 90s background music comes to a merciful end. "This is Paul from FastFeast, where you get your food in twenty minutes or it's on us. How can I help you?"

"Hi, I need to get some information on one of your drivers, Patricia Hayes," I say, flipping my paper over to the blank side. "She was found—"

"If you want to make a complaint about a driver, you have to do it through the app or on our website," Paul interrupts. His voice is a nasal, dismissive drone on par with a half-crushed wasp. "If you're having trouble with the app, I'll redirect you to—"

"I don't have a complaint. She's dead."

He pauses, then clicks his tongue. "Well, I can't do anything about that, sir."

The call ends, leaving me with a piercing dial tone and a knot of irritation between my eyebrows. "Thanks."

I try another number listed for the app, but it puts me in a never-ending telephone tree. The tenth time I'm told to press one, I give up and call the rideshare company instead. Chewing through another semi-soy Super Energy bar provides an outlet for my boredom as I listen to Chauffeur's ad spiel on loop, waiting for a connection.

The cycle of misery ends when a cheery voice kicks in. "Hi! You've reached the Chauffeur private helpline. This is Melinda. How can I assist you?"

"Hello. I was looking for someone that could talk to me about Patricia Hayes. She was one of your drivers."

"If you have a complaint—"

Fuck's sake. "Can you just connect me to your manager?"

I'm expecting pushback, but maybe she's worried about getting caught in the aura of a one-star review, because after a pregnant pause, Melinda says, "I'll transfer you right now, ma'am. Thanks for calling the Chauffeur helpline!"

Phone calls irk me for plenty of reasons, but the misgendering ouroboros has to be at the top of the list. "Thanks."

Irritation pulls my teeth out of groove, making them grind, but I can't give someone stapled to a company line too much flak. If I had to answer calls from dawn to dusk over cold fries and busted tail lights, I'd be slamming my head into the keyboard by customer number five.

After a few rings, the manager finally picks up. "This is Deja. How can I be of assistance?"

Let the third time be the charm. "Hi. I'm calling to report the death of one of your drivers. Patricia Hayes."

"I see. I'm sorry to hear that." Her regret sounds genuine, and a couple of quick key taps follow. "We processed forty-seven dollars and sixteen cents into her account yesterday, including tips and tax. I'll have the full amount transferred to Patricia's bank account and close out her profile."

If Nikki can have the city get access to those funds, they'll probably go straight to the cremation. Which is a bonus, but not what I was looking for. "I was actually trying to track her last known whereabouts. Did she log any trips on Sunday?"

"Are you calling on behalf of the family?" Deja asks.

A more diplomatic way of asking whether or not I'm a cop. "Yeah. I'm afraid her husband also passed away."

"I'm sorry, we can't hand over any data without a warrant." She sighs. "I know, it's not fair. I've taken dozens of calls like this over the last few years. Even the folks doing contract tracing hit a brick wall from corporate."

Well, shit. At least she's being honest with me. Maybe I can ask Nikki if she found Patricia's phone instead, crack it open, and work backwards. I mostly want to know if she ran into trouble on the way home.

"All right. Anything else you can tell me?"

"She had a five-star rating. Beyond that, no." After a bit more typing, she adds, "The money's been sent. And please, pass on my condolences."

There's no one to pass them to except Nikki, but I won't say that and make this woman's day worse. "Sure thing. Thank you."

I would kill for a clean high right now. Something sweet and quick, straight to the skull to scrub out my tension. Shame the blood won't let me. A fucked-up glimpse in my dreams is the only thing I'm going to get, the promise of temptation with no possible delivery.

With Patricia's leads stalled out, I move on to Scott. His shop is eight blocks away, and I'd rather walk the streets than make another phone call. People tend to be a lot more forthcoming when you can look them in the eye, anyway.

I get dressed and head downstairs. Halfway past the co-op, I spy a white Ford Fusion with a parking ticket jammed against the windshield. The license plate matches what the Hayes's put down for the apartment.

After shredding the ticket—what are they going to do, sue the dead?—I peek into the car to make sure nothing interesting is hiding inside.

Their sedan is at least ten years old, age exposed in worn black seats and cracked plastic throughout the interior. Everything is clean as can be, though, along with a Chauffeur safety disclaimer zip-tied to the back of the driver's seat. The car has a few accidents to its name, highlighted by a brand new bumper surrounded with factory-era paint, and one side mirror in smooth, reflective shape next to its dull twin.

I check the doors just in case, but as expected, they're locked. Working a tool into the trunk to wrench it open wouldn't be hard, but I'm not a professional carjacker—the alarm would go off. Considering the stripped emptiness of Scott and Patricia's apartment, I imagine that if they ever kept anything of value stored back here it was sold off a long time ago.

Playing with the bits of ticket paper in my pocket gives my hands something to do on the way to the mechanic. The sky is a blur of cement gray, a gust kicking up in maddened bursts whenever there's a gap between buildings. Chicago sits on a true city grid, which means intersections become wind tunnels every time the breeze darts in the right direction. It dries out the asphalt in winter, leaving long lesions between old black joints, ready to bulge and split under pressure.

Mateo's Auto Repair sits fenced in alongside a parking lot, big enough for customers and junkers-in-progress alike. The man himself is trying to light a cigarette with a matchbook outside the front door, muttering a curse in Portuguese when the match head flames out, charred and useless.

He looks up in surprise when I offer my lighter. "Hey, thanks."

"No problem." A quick once-over doesn't reveal anything out of the ordinary. His navy jumpsuit is spotted with oil old and new, and four kinds of pens are sticking out from the pocket below his stained name tag. "I'm going to take a wild guess and assume you own this place."

"Well, my dad founded this place, but yeah. Now it's mine." Mateo smiles before confusion creases his brow. "You don't seem to have a car. How can I help you?"

"I was looking for information on Scott Hayes," I say.

His face falls, and Mateo takes a long drag from the cigarette. "God, I guess he really is dead. Scott's landlady called to tell me the other day, but it hadn't sunk in yet."

Nikki would blow a fuse at being called a landlady, but most folks aren't keyed into the co-op system, so I let it slide. "You two get along, then?"

"I mean, yeah, of course. Scott started working here right after he finished school. Honestly, he was more of a front desk and parts guy rather than a mechanic, but I made sure to teach him the ropes whenever there was a chance."

Mateo is twitchy. The movements are subtle—double blinks and the slow crush of his cigarette between drags, his other thumb working circles against the inner seam of a pocket. I can't guess what he's so nervous about, but there's one way to pull out the truth.

I press my own thumb hard against the pulse in my wrist, deep enough to bruise. As it throbs, steady and slow, I listen for Mateo's heartbeat, feeling for where it falls into sync. His rhythm is taut and quick right now, blood rushing in and out like a 3 a.m. joyrider.

"Was Scott in any kind of trouble?" I ask, still attuned.

Mateo's pulse answers like a snare drum, *tap tap tap*. "No. I mean, not that I ever heard about. Didn't have any kind of arrest record when I hired him."

Then why is Scott's boss lying through his teeth? "Mateo, I'm not a cop. Not a private eye or anything like that either. So if he was having an issue with drugs, or Patricia, or—"

"Jesus, nothing like that," Mateo mutters. "Patricia dropped him off at work every day, then picked him up too, unless they were having the car worked on. She even brought him an extra lunch if someone didn't come out to claim the food she was delivering."

Thready, but even. Now we're getting somewhere. "I know bills were tight for them. You sure he wasn't making any cash on the side?"

Even if I wasn't playing wiretap with his heartbeat, the way Mateo's eyes widen prove I'm right on the money. "It *wasn't* drugs. I don't see how it could have anything to do with this, I swear."

"I'm not here to rat you out, man." I couldn't care less about someone's side hustle, unless they're stealing plasma from orphans or something. "But Scott died bad. If there could be any connection, I have to know."

Mateo snubs out his cigarette, shoulders tripwire tight. "It was metal. Copper pipe, brass fittings. The kind of scrap that pulls a premium at the yard. I let him borrow a couple tools out of the shop to go collecting."

Scott doesn't strike me as the type of guy to go raiding downtown construction sites in the middle of the night. "Collecting where?"

"The South side," Mateo admits, guilt rounding his eyes. "Most of the empty houses there have been picked over, but with a good electric saw, you can cut down to the stuff that's worth a bit of money."

"South side's big. Where, exactly?"

"Englewood, thereabouts."

I can't imagine anyone living around there would take kindly to some random white guy tearing up abandoned houses, but I can't see them killing him for it either. Especially not the way he and Patricia went out. "He ever get caught?"

"Not that I know of." Mateo shrugs. "I don't even do it myself, okay? Scott came begging, asking if I had any way for him to make an extra dime. Something where no one would get hurt. It was all I could come up with."

I raise a brow. Stripping supplies from one of the most segregated neighborhoods in the city isn't exactly harmless. "Giving him extra shifts was out of the question?"

"Times are lean." Discomfort lingers on Mateo's face, a curved line tugging at his cheek. "Plenty of people ditched their cars for good when they went remote. Weren't using them. Keeping one in the city is too damn expensive."

He has a point. I've never owned a car, even when there happened to be enough cash in my lap to afford one. The train takes me anywhere I want to go, and the nearest Red Line station is a stone's throw from the apartment. Scott and Patricia would have been on the hook for insurance and parking on top of everything else, or she'd lose both of her jobs.

"And Scott didn't say anything unusual the last time you saw him? Nothing that stands out now?"

Mateo shakes his head. "I threw him a couple hours on Saturday. It was the nasty work, cleaning oil pans and gummed-up equipment, but Scott never complained. Patricia picked him up like usual, and that was that."

Sure would be nice if the Hayes's were even a fraction less normal. "Okay. I appreciate you talking to me."

"No worries. Wish I could have been more helpful."

My stomach growls, insistent. The pair of soy bars weren't enough. "You could tell me where there's something good to eat around here."

He directs me to a kebab shop on the next block. Ordering a plate of doner sets me back a few bucks, but the perpetual meat carousel is too tempting to turn down.

I'm settled in with my carved plate of bliss when my phone buzzes with a call. The screen says it's Nikki, which is odd—she knows better than anyone else how much I hate talking on the phone.

I pick up anyway. "Hello?"

"Cam, where are you?"

She sounds out of breath, distracted. I lean against the restaurant window to try and read the name, but it's in Turkish. "Down south a few blocks. I was checking up on Scott's workplace. What's going on?"

"The whole block is swarmed with cops. There's a body hanging out the window."

This is getting ridiculous. "Our side of the block?"

"No, across the street. A rich lady from Wilmette was out walking her prize corgi, saw someone dangling dead up from the fourth floor. I think her scream scared half the neighborhood."

Explains why so many cops showed up. Upsetting the kind of people who fund the yearly police ball is bad optics. "You think it's related to Scott and Patricia?"

"I don't know. What I do know is that it looks like our murder per capita rate is going up by the day, and I need to know why."

I could push back against Nikki calling this 'murder', but I don't actually think she's wrong. There was nothing natural about what I saw in that apartment, and bodies don't usually fall out of windows by accident. "I'll get back down there and check it out. Stay safe, okay?"

"You too. CPD's sure to be in a pissy mood."

Hell freezes over when one of those ghouls starts smiling. "Don't worry. You know me. I'm a people person."

Nikki laughs before saying goodbye.

I stare down at what's left of my food, make a gamble, and start wolfing the rest down. Clearing my plate is a compulsion; my mother broke her back to give me three square meals, but with inflation, it was more like one and a half.

My father skipped out before I could walk, saddling her with twenty grand of credit card debt and a precocious toddler. With age, one truth claimed me down to the bone—I would do whatever it took to never, ever feel that clench in my gut again. Not a crumb or sip gets left behind, even if it's old, dry, rotten.

So hopefully whatever's going on at home won't make me toss this all back up.

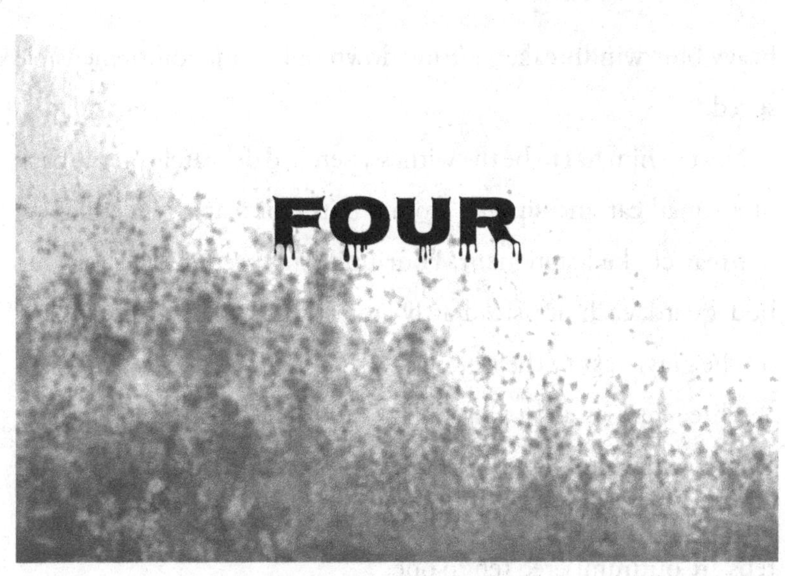

FOUR

Swarm is an understatement.

A whole filthy hive of Chicago police chokes out Ashland, their steady line of red and blue lights turning every pair of mirrored sunglasses into flickering compound eyes. Crime scene tape stretches from the front of the building and across the sidewalk fence, warding off passerby and keeping the residents corralled inside. I don't see any hard Kevlar shells signaling the SWAT squad, but this isn't that kind of threat. It's the dramatic but presently harmless sort that lets every officer here stand in place and rack up extra hours on the local dime.

Giving the front of the apartment a wide berth, I stick close to the corner fencing as I can, hoping the willowy trees hanging over the sharp black bars provide enough cover. Another careful scan of the area turns up who I expected to see: a homicide detective in his heavy blue windbreaker, jotting down notes at incomprehensible speed.

Next to him has to be the witness, perched delicately on the back of a squad car and sipping from a bottle of water while making her tear-choked statement. Four uniforms are with her playing bodyguard, each one steadfastly ignoring the wiggly corgi pissing on the grass next to their boots.

Three guesses as to why Nikki didn't get the same treatment. Even her being alderwoman doesn't tip the balance much; cops don't care about the political types here unless the police union reps are outnumbered ten to one.

"Terry started barking, and I was trying to keep him quiet, because he knows it's really not polite to be loud in other people's neighborhoods—" The lady from Wilmette sniffles, then wipes the tears from round green eyes; her makeup is expensive enough not to smear. "But I looked up and saw... he was just trying to keep me safe."

The detective nods like her panicked saga is going to make the front page of the Tribune, but if she's not local, I doubt she knows anything relevant about what's going on. A quick check confirms the cops on scene are either looking at her or glaring at the sidewalk, so I follow the witness' directions, tracing along the building until the first drops of blood start to show.

Like Nikki said, the victim was on the fourth floor, but a long spill of red has made it down to the third, coalescing into a puddle at the broad top of the sill. The body isn't visible anymore—the cops must have pulled it up to hide the eyesore—but only an industrial level cleaner could scale the complex and scour the brick, never mind replacing the gouged out window. The break wasn't clean; huge pieces of scarlet glass spiderwebbed with cracks lay by the fence. Whoever went through the window hit it hard first, before a second push broke the last point of resistance.

That means at least two people involved, same as Scott and Patricia. I can't be sure they're connected unless I see the bodies, which is going to be difficult since the police actually stuck around this time.

There *is* a lot of blood on the windowsill, though. I might be able to tap a vein and see how far it goes, confirm if there's more than one body inside the apartment. Syncing up is ten times harder at a distance, but strolling into an active crime scene isn't really an option.

I slip out my lancet and poke a fingertip, deep enough for a heavy red bead to bubble to the surface. Rubbing it together against my thumb provides more surface area, and I stare as it spreads, trying to unfocus my vision and forget about everything but the blood. The problem with not knowing how any of this shit works is that I'm not very good at it. I might as well be trying to fit together wires by color in a pitch black room while someone slowly shoves a needle into my brain.

The stains on the brick are out of reach, and getting older by the second. Every beat of my heart is a slow crawl upward, hand over hand, finding footholds in the last glimmers of life soaked into the wall. A dull throb builds behind my right eye, swelling with the aggrieved arrogance of a tumor, trying to push out its lessers. I bite my tongue until that bleeds too; focusing is easier when copper is the only thing I can taste.

Whoever toppled out of the window is on the floor of the apartment now, flat and spread-eagle. The corpse rings a cold note next to the bodies moving around inside, hot and heavy pulses beating through my head like someone struck my eardrum with a hammer. If I listen too hard, I can hear the hearts of everyone around me. I only made that mistake once, and spent the day sobbing on the floor with both hands clutched at my head, trying to tune out too much life in too little space, each beat out of rhythm but thunderously loud.

There's a second corpse. Maybe five feet past the first one, yet just as rigid, which means the cops didn't shoot an assailant on entry. Half my suspicions are confirmed, but this unconventional dowsing is far too imprecise to give me any idea of how they died, if there are pieces of them missing, or if anyone else was there who didn't happen to bleed.

So I go try the other direction, tracing the blood back down the building, looking for something fresh. The stain breaks on the brick and catches again on the busted glass, but I feel something low and stagnant down below, further than I expect. Not the sidewalk—underneath the dark crust of the street, clinging to the pipes. Stretching to the other side of the block where Scott and Patricia died.

Is this the same thing? Did it spread?

"What the fuck are you doing?"

A broad hand grabs the collar of my jacket and pulls so hard I get whiplash. The world spins in echoes of red, flashing like club lights as my brain tries to reconcile physical reality with a sudden shift in perspective. On the upside, it overrides my reflex to resist; the downside is I'm looking in the face of a Chicago police officer who appears none too pleased to see me. He's not the one who grabbed me, though. His partner must be the one with a leech's grip on the leather at my back.

"Nothing," I manage to say. My tongue moves like a slug, wet and heavy in my mouth. "Just wanted to know what's going on."

He—no idea on the name, since convenient bands of black elastic wrap around his badge number and ID card—stares at me like I extended him the Nobel Peace Prize. After dealing with enough cops, the fact that their eyes are shrouded by sunglasses doesn't mean very much; their rage at being challenged shows from head to toe, without a hint of subtlety to be found.

"You high?" He—let's go with This Asshole—asks me.

If only. "No, officer. I'm not high."

A mustached lip curls back in open disdain. "Uh-huh. How about you show me some identification and explain why there's blood on your hands?"

"I pricked my finger." Turning it back and forth for him to see makes his partner—That Asshole—tighten his hold on my jacket. "Is that a crime?"

"Identification." This Asshole sounds out every syllable, which would be more intimidating if he didn't come off like a Sunday school teacher running the spelling bee. "Now."

"Wallet's in my left pocket," I say, waiting a beat before reaching into my joggers and pulling out the folded lump of leather. My blood pulses with anger, a hot pressure straining every vein like pipes waiting to burst.

He yanks the wallet out of my grip before I can offer anything up, blatantly rifling through the inner pocket. The wallet is crowded with receipts and a single five dollar bill, which he observes with a grunt of open amusement. This Asshole yanks my state ID out of its narrow plastic window and holds it up to the light.

"Cameron Ciris. '91. Lives across the street."

I love when cops know my address. Really makes my day.

"What's this *X* shit?" He demands, nostrils flaring wide with disgust.

This Asshole's head tilts, peering over silver lenses and below my belt. It takes everything in me not to drive my knee into that slack jaw of his so hard teeth crash through the chamber of his skull. It takes even more than that not to blow every capillary in stark blue eyes, making me the last thing he ever sees. I could, if I ever let this *thing* out of me.

Cops are the white-beats-Black binary monstrosity infesting every city. If you don't fit in the ever-shifting lines of what they consider harmless, they kill you. The only reason I'm not already face-first in asphalt is because This Asshole and I happen to share the same pale shell, but any implied solidarity is temporary. CPD will shoot anyone in the back of the head if they're bored or annoyed enough.

"What do you think, partner?" He asks That Asshole, who has decided to squeeze my arms together like a seafood cracker. "Disturbing the peace? A couple hours in lockup will prove my point nicely."

Holding my tongue burns, but I have no choice. Every minute I'm in a cell keeps me further from the truth, and I can't burden Nikki with a bail call neither of us can afford. She's already cobbling together every last penny to get the Hayes's final affairs settled.

"You kidding?" His partner grunts. "I don't want this freak in the back of my car. We just got it cleaned after the last ride."

Sometimes revulsion wears a mask shaped like mercy.

That Asshole lets go. Pins and needles flood my forearms, blood going back where it should be. I call even more to my fingertips, ready to make a blackout-heavy fist if they suddenly change their minds. My disassembled wallet is dropped unceremoniously back into my palm, and I flinch to keep the ID from slipping to the ground.

This Asshole looks me up and down, then nods. "Yeah, whatever. Just don't let me see your face around again any time soon."

"Get the fuck out of here." That Asshole orders, pushing two fingers between my shoulder blades. "You got ten seconds."

The cop in front cracks a grin at me, hands dropping to his duty belt and presenting a clear choice between pistol and taser. Rather than entertain his private show, I walk back across the street, ignore my apartment, and keep going. There's no chance in hell I'm going to hole up in there after they spiked my info, especially if Mr. Homicide up front goes sweeping for suspects.

Six blocks later, my heartbeat cools back down, although the ache in my elbows has yet to fade. Anger frays at my mind like a razor against the grain, working my nerves raw and driving the sting even deeper. The blood would have let me tear those cops apart, flay them open with a twist of the wrist. That truth has sat next to me for a long time, waiting for me to take its hand when the time is right. But the urge to pop their carotids like gut-swollen mosquitoes wars with the notion that knowing how to start doesn't give me any clue on how to stop.

And dicing up two uniforms isn't enough. The rest would be after me before you can say 9-1-1. I'd have to kill them all; I'd have to turn the whole world red.

Sometimes, I think about doing it anyway.

A diner is the first place I find where it's socially acceptable to sit down and decompress. The host points me to an empty booth in the back with seats the color of a second day bruise, purple and a bit too swollen with stuffing to sit against comfortably. I turn over the laminated menu a couple of times, pretending to make a decision before a server comes my way.

She flips her order pad open to a new page. "Hey, I'm Jane and I'll be taking care of you today. Need more time or are you ready to order?"

For the sake of my wallet, it's tempting to just order coffee, but a lot of places get annoyed if you sit too long nursing refills. "I saw something about a soup of the day. What kind are we talking about?"

Jane's smile is white and plastic, molded in place. "Italian dinner! Sausage, ravioli, a whole lot of tomatoes and cheese. How's that sound?"

Sounds like food. "Okay. I'll take that. Along with some ice water and a cup of dark roast, if you don't mind."

"You got it." After a swift black scrawl on the pad, she steps away and into the kitchen, falling out of sight.

The drinks come fast, so I use them to occupy my hands and try to shrug off the feeling that someone's right behind me. I never leaned paranoid when I was high, but sober life has given me plenty of reasons to look over my shoulder. Part of the puzzle was being too blitzed to care—ignorance really can be bliss.

I watch traffic through the window while fiddling with the sugar and cream until the server comes back with a steaming bowl of soup. It's much bigger than I expected, forcing her to gingerly put it down with both hands on the table.

She sweeps up my mug on the way back. "I'll fill this up from the fresh pot."

"Thanks," I say, picking up my spoon and digging deep.

Patricia Hayes's dull green eye stares back at me from a cradle of red-tinged silver. The optic nerve trails in shredded, delicate threads down to the blood it was birthed from, where fragments of teeth float, adrift.

"What the—"

Anger wars with disgust in my chest as I jerk my eyes away to demand an explanation, but Jane is already standing there. Every vein in her body is frostbite blue, a nest of thrashing and twisting snakes desperate to slip their skin. Her eyes are gone, leaving behind sockets slick as cherry pits, open like a sacrificial offering. A too-wide smile bares pristine molars, shining and surrounded by taut muscle.

"...fuck."

I shove the bowl and spoon away from me, trying to get some distance—to get out of the damn booth—but the hard shatter of ceramic on tile throws a wrench in the works. Sharp white pieces cover the floor, just like—

"Are you okay?"

Blinking twice, I process the warm hand against my shoulder before daring to look up again. The server is staring at me—she has eyes now, gas fire blue without a hint of green—with a wary mix of fear and concern.

Rightfully so, because it seems like I just sent half my food flying and startled her bad enough to drop my cup.

Flashbacks aren't new to me. Old trips crop back up as an inevitable side effect when you do enough acid, but there's a huge goddamn difference between seeing stars in streetlights and this saw-toothed hallucination. I have no excuse for lashing out, but I need one, and fast.

"I'm so sorry," I say, fitting together the first lie that comes to mind. "A friend of mine just died. It's really been messing with me."

I gauge a fifty-fifty chance she kicks me out of the diner, but at the last second, sympathy takes hold. Jane's hand falls away, reaching for the towel tucked in the band of her apron. Her smile is sad, but a lot less forced as she starts mopping up the soup I spilled across the table.

"You're not the first person to tell me that this week," she says. Guilt makes my stomach lurch; I've never met a corpse that was close to me. "I swear, this city gets in a mood sometimes. Like there's something in the water."

"And it's not even summer," I murmur.

Murder is a known affair in this city, but it spikes with the heat. Cook together enough humid misery with boiling asphalt and violence blooms like mold, bursting out of every neglected crack and frustrated fracture. When the world works so hard to try and kill you, it's hard to blame people for wanting to get in a few shots of their own. I wonder if the streets ever get tired of swallowing pain and decide to spit something back out, something just as hateful and targeted as the blood punched deep into pavement.

Once the table's clean, I dare to look back down at the half-empty bowl. Nothing's in it but tomato soup with chunks of pasta and pale sausage floating near the surface, little flecks of basil and thyme flavoring the meat.

What the hell is wrong with me?

"Can I help you clean up?" I gesture to the busted mug. Certain places have strict rules about that sort of thing, in case a customer sues because a piece of glass goes under their nailbed or something. "It's kind of my day job."

"Oh, it's fine. I'll grab the broom and sweep it in one go." Jane gently pushes the bowl back my way. "Try and eat. You'll feel better with something in your stomach."

Despite the answering roil in my gut, I pick up the spoon again.

I'm half-tempted to text Nikki about the things I'm seeing, if only to have a record on hand. Hallucinations are like dreams, slipping away the second you think about them too hard. But what do I say to her?

From the top—

Hi, Nikki. As you know, I used to do enough cocaine to assassinate half of Wall Street. It would be lovely if you could remind me of this on the off-chance I turn up howling mad outside your doorstep thanks to my defunct brain chemistry. Love, Cameron.

Yeah, fuck that.

Lukewarm soup doesn't stir anyone's appetite, and mine already fled out the back alley five minutes ago. But until every drop is gone, I can't leave. At least the mechanics are simple: scoop, chew, swallow. I wish it tasted a bit less like tomato-soaked cardboard, but that's not the line cook's fault. My senses are wired up like a rat king's tail.

I eat until the spoon scrapes the bottom of the bowl, then leave a fifty percent tip and duck out the front before the server and I can lock eyes again. Some of the edge from earlier with the cops has worn off, but not enough. Going to see Katherine and get my mind off things would be ideal, but it's already ticked past seven.

Which means a shower and getting ready for work. I would call in sick, but the other janitor at Xanthous with my certifications has a kid to look after—all by himself, no less. Ryan only works part-time anyway, covering nights that I'm off and sharing an over-lap shift on Saturdays.

I'll survive. What's a little more blood after a day like this?

FIVE

My **nightly routine is** pretty straightforward. I start with all of the clinic's RMW—read: biohazard—bins, triple-checking that nothing has poked or soaked through the bags. Then I slip on a fresh case around each one, tie it off, and bring everything to the locked dumpster out back. Regulation says I have to relock the dumpster after every disposal, even if I'm just stepping back inside for a single forgotten bin. Xanthous could get sued fifty ways to Sunday if someone curious got exposed from any on-site waste, or worse, if a stalker got ahold of a patient's DNA via misappropriated samples.

You know when they make a law like that, it's because of some truly heinous shit. I never asked for context, because I don't want the details.

EDM pours through my headphones as I knot together a few more bags and haul them outside. I've always been a sucker for good beats and seductive nonsense disguising itself as lyrics. *Breathing in gods, na na na.* Love it.

Except I can't get my fix from the clubs anymore, even though they've reopened. The raves that wandered underground during quarantine are back in new buildings, with new DJs and promises of easy oblivion. Sure, getting high is out of the question, but there are other complications. Whoever survived, whoever recognized me, would be sure to ask questions I can't answer: *Where have you been, Cameron? How did someone like you get sober? What happened to your dealer?*

So no old haunts for me. Not today, and not tomorrow.

The whole trash process is Sisyphean—unlock the door from the inside, set everything down by the dumpster, then lock the door behind me until the dumpster's closed again—but the clinic roof is riddled with cameras, and I'd get fired the first time anyone noticed me propping the back entrance open to speed things up.

Not that I'm in a rush. The best part about this job is that no one's looking over my shoulder, giving orders, or sending emails. Eight hours of lifting and moving keeps me in better shape than my half-assed attempts at the gym ever did, and it's hard to fuck things up when I do the exact same thing every night of the week.

Yet my stomach grumbles, caustic with need. I've eaten more in the last few days than I usually do in weeks, despite my stomach's regular rebellion. All the restaurant food is probably to blame. Next thing I know, it'll be demanding caviar.

As I head back inside, the lock resets with an electric chirp. Its stark green light fades away, and I hear the sound of something dripping past my earbuds. My mop is where I left it, leaning in its bucket against the wall, so that can't be the source.

Why aren't you looking at me, Cameron?

I freeze. The song keeps going, loud bass weaving together in a drop that vibrates through my entire skull. After a deep breath, I pinpoint the new sound around the corner, and lean out into the hall.

Katherine is floating above the floor, staring at me—through me. A gloss of silver mist, barely a face, the chalk outline shape of a body.

See, see, see, see—

I rip out my headphones. Without the chopped vocals, my heartbeat is ten times louder, a steady hammer against fragile ribs.

"You can't be here," I whisper. "There's no blood."

Her smile is an uneven crescent, eyes wide and manic. "Oh, of course there's blood, honey. You're here. A walking wound—every city has one. The next gash in a line that's been cutting through this place since 1780."

This isn't her. A pink tinge clings to the mist, getting redder by the second. Katherine melts into something clinging and red, sticky hands reaching for my boots. I hate that my fucked-up brain chemistry can conjure the woman I love in such perfect detail, that temptation dares to wear her face, stealing a part of Kat away from me too.

Then she's gone, and I'm staring at the tile I scrubbed spotless just an hour ago.

"I've been inside you for so long." The voice suddenly drips between my ears, water torture via bone conduction. "Why aren't you listening?"

Something heavy and wet slaps against the floor in the other hall. A squelching drag of damp flesh on tile, as if someone's having a seizure in the shower. Clawing, grasping, twitching for balance.

"Okay," I mutter. "What now?"

One of the worst parts about hallucinations is knowing they're not real doesn't change much. Logic is about as helpful as a CAUTION sign next to a derailing train. The only thing to do is try and chill out until whatever synapses are going haywire get too tired to conjure up anything else. Except relaxing is a lost cause when they're fucking with my music.

Seeing things is unsettling, but hearing shit is worse. Sound digs into the brain, invisible but possessing its own invasive shape. When the next slick noise is interrupted by a sharp snap—like a stick, or bone—irritation bids me to yank my mop and bin down to the other hall, purposefully splashing the water inside around.

"You like that, huh? I can make a racket too," I snap. "Shut up already."

Sure, arguing with myself has never gotten very far, but I'm tired. I want to finish my shift, collapse into bed, and hope the sludge of exhaustion wipes out any brewing nightmares. When push comes to shove, I'll take the distant, empty gray over anything else.

The sound suddenly stops, as if someone cut a cord to a speaker. I wait ten seconds, then peer around the far corner.

A corpse is sprawled out on the tile, the light above him flickering. His throat is shredded to a meaty cavity, but it's not Scott. This man is older and Black, with dots from old medical IVs forming a raised constellation inside one elbow. Someone else is crouched over him, one hand buried to the slick red wrist. I recognize the cross-studded shirt from my dream before its wearer looks up at me with a craterous abyss for eyes, and a sloppy, dripping mouth.

No, not a mouth. It reminds me of a whale I saw on a documentary at 2 a.m., hairy plates of baleen pulling in offal like a sieve. Slippery bristles twitch, scenting the air, and it—*he*—lunges forward, leapfrogging over the body towards me.

All I have is the damn mop. The handle deflects the first messy bite towards my face, but his bloody fingers catch around the wood. He shoves hard enough to slam my head into the wall, mop crushed lengthwise against my throat. I wheeze, vision narrowed to flashing holes of black, white, and mocking scarlet. The arms pinning me are soft and swollen with rot, but no matter how much

I thrash, there's no give. Even a hard knee between the legs offers nothing but the squish of overripe fruit.

That awful maw scrapes past the collar of my jacket, seeking my mouth. I try to clench my jaw, brace my teeth, but they're wrenched apart. Something small and hard drops onto my tongue: a single, bitter seed. When the handle at my throat eases, I choke on my next breath and swallow. It sticks, suddenly liquid and hot. My knees buckle.

As I sag to the floor, the last thing I see is that wet red hand rising to scrawl a symbol on the wall.

I'm freezing.

Cold radiates through my spine, joints locked tight. The only hint of warmth is in the back of my skull, pulsing with dull, distant agony. Flexing my fingers confirms ten are still attached, and one by one I count my limbs: present and accounted for. Opening my eyes is the hardest part, a thousand tempting hands trying to drag me back into the unconscious sea. The effort is barely worth it—there's nothing to see but the rugged white popcorn of Xanthous Medical's ceiling.

"Fuck," I mutter, pushing at the floor to try and sit up.

My palms skid over wet tile, but the jolt of adrenaline that follows jerks me up just in time. After a few seconds, the knockoff gaussian blur screwing with my vision dissipates. Both mop and basin are knocked over at my feet, water from the latter drenching the floor. Everything from my jacket to my shoes is drenched.

This isn't the first time I've woken up on my back with dry mouth and a killer headache, but definitely it's the first time I've done it at work.

I don't find a body in the hall, or any signs that one was ever there. Not a single drop of blood either, even when I reach to touch the sore spot at the back of my head. The swelling throbs, stinging at the slightest contact, but nothing seems to be broken. Katherine is going to be pissed that I dropkicked my brain twice in a week, though.

She's not here, she can't be, but I still call out loud, "Kat? Did you come to see me?"

Silence answers, and I can't complain. One of the best things about our relationship is how hard it is for me to fuck her over. She's already dead, which substantially limits any damage I can do. Creeping her out, however, still remains a possibility.

Getting to my knees is slow work, punctuated by the squish of sodden denim. Setting the basin upright doesn't fix much, but tossing the mop back in puts a little more order in the world. Despite the knot of pain lingering in my skull, I stand up without so much as a dizzy spell. The wall behind me is a clean seafoam green, same as always. Psych books say the color is soothing, but that spotless paint sends anger pouring through my body, toxic as mercury. No sigil, no blood, just a bunch of sad gray water.

Was all that shit fake? First the cafe, now my damn job. I shouldn't be spiraling when I'm this clean. Why am I falling apart so fast?

I mean, besides the obvious.

Now I have to get the backup mop to dry off the floor, and finish my shift without so much as an aspirin. The thought alone sets my mind ablaze with frustration, but it's either that or giving up my job tomorrow. If anyone working here—or worse, a client—slips because of a wet spot, getting fired would be the best case scenario.

And I only have two hours to finish everything, because according to the wall clock, I was down and out for nearly half my shift. The only saving grace is a lack of confidentiality-violating cameras inside the building, so my dead fish impression on the floor went unrecorded.

Without any music, mopping up is a slog, but I won't risk triggering that loop in my brain a second time. By the time I leave, my body feels like it's breaking off at the welds, and my clothes still aren't dry. Chicago wind eats layers for breakfast, sneaking in through every soggy spot of cloth, tenacious as a locust.

Cigarettes make for piss-poor hand warmers, but they'll have to do. Glass crunches when I unzip my jacket pocket, and irritation boils inside me with the malice of cheap city tar before I gingerly reach inside and feel around for the damage. My lighter is just fine on top, but one of the vials is in a dozen pieces; it must have happened with the fall. The others seem to be intact, including the one with my sample from Scott. I take the tube out and hold it up to the streetlight, looking for any cracks.

Stringy brown threads grow along the inside of the glass, stretching up to the hermetically sealed cap. Thick, leaf-like veins leech from the blood like a straw, clotting in a mossy sponge at the very bottom.

"The hell is this?" I turn the vial over, watching for any movement, but it seems as inert as any plant. Whatever the substance, it holds to the glass like glue, resisting any attempts to budge when I give the glass a hard shake.

Blood doesn't mold. When it's dry enough, blood barely does anything. Even the diseases everyone worries about, be it hepatitis or HIV, don't have the knack to survive outside the human body for very long. Gas gangrene is horrifying, stomach-bursting shit, but that requires an entire corpse; an arterial spill is nowhere near enough.

Maybe the Hayes's *were* sick. Just not with something Nikki or I were looking for.

I need to go to the second scene. If the people who died across the street were killed by the same thing, then this isn't just lethal—it's contagious. The weather app on my phone promises a gray morning; I have thirty minutes before sunrise. While the twenty-four hour mark hasn't passed yet, I'd wager CPD didn't fancy pulling third shift outside a blood-drenched room. Cops are squeamish about carnage they're not responsible for. If they're gone, I can get in.

Pre-dawn puts the city in a dream state. After the parties have ended and the bars close, but before anyone with a hangover is up hunting for something greasy. There's not even sirens at this hour, only a cool fall mist that carries on the wind like the city's somnolent breath. Despite the chill biting at my bones, the tension bleeds out of my shoulders. If I blur my eyes a bit, I can pretend Katherine's waiting for me in the fog off Clark.

My block is silent too. The cops already stripped away their yellow tape, leaving nothing behind but a couple of oil slicks from ill-maintained cruisers. No one's around to stop me from walking through the front gate, or taking advantage of the fact that whoever cut the locks on this block made them answer to the same key. I slip in the front, listening for boots or jangling duty belts, but the only noise is someone's radiator working overtime.

The crime theater outside is gone, but the active scene red tape is everywhere on the fourth floor. This X is stretched out wide and high, bullying the doors of two other apartments, as if the cops thought evidence might walk out through the walls. Said cops aren't here protecting or serving, so I duck through the open door. Protocol demands they keep an entrance propped to avoid new fingerprints, which is hilarious considering how much evidence the department ruins on any given day.

I flick on the light. White plastic markers divide the hardwood floor into a diagram of tragedy, highlighting two misshapen outlines of blood. The first reaches to the window, where a half-inch thick crust crowds the windowsill. A few dry footprints present a confusing puzzle—whoever made them was facing where the second body fell, then booked it over to the glass. The window is unlocked, but they headbutt their way through instead of sliding it up and open. What jagged pieces remain are clouded with equal parts blood and fat, a less than subtle impalement, gut-deep.

Why go there to begin with? If they were running, wouldn't the door have made more sense?

Animal panic is as good a reason as any, but it doesn't explain the stains around the second corpse. In the middle of the room, where there's a gap in the mess, I follow a palm-wide blood trail where it smears up the kitchen cabinet, spills across the counter, and dives back down into the stainless steel sink. The Hayes's sink looked almost identical, although Scott had a lot less ground to cover.

Underneath the pervasive odor of death and chemistry—luminol, nothing fun—is something stale and rotten. A few more steps into the kitchen gives away the culprits: a shredded package of bacon decaying to pale slime next to an upside-down cereal box. Mashed spheres of cornmeal litter the space in front of the fridge, like someone went and loaded up on carbs before the slaughter.

I check the other cabinets; they're near to bursting. The one big difference between this place and the Hayes's—besides square footage—is there's actual food in this house. They even had a grocery list written on custom paper, surrounded by leaves and illustrated vegetables. Whoever lived here was fifty feet away from Scott and Patricia, but experiencing an entirely different notion of existence.

These folks weren't hungry. Yet by the look of it, the two of them tore each other up the exact same way. Save the window, the rest of the apartment is intact: even an opportunistic murderer would have snagged the silver bracelet resting in a bowl on the living room table, surrounded by spare change and crumpled bills. The cops were the fools who left the front door open; the lock is perfectly intact.

Leaving all this blood unidentified feels wrong. I had checked local news on my way to work, scrounging for information, but only found a minor note about a 'disturbance' on our street. Sometimes the cops play coy when they suspect a pattern, but this reeks of a cover-up. If anyone found out they don't have an answer to four people on the same block ripping each other up within seventy-two hours, putting a light on the subject would cause a panic.

Needing the truth turns me back into a scavenger. I find a collection of spam mail abandoned by the door belonging to Ellis and

Ricardo North; the invitation to renew their vows at Palm Beach marks them as husbands instead of relatives.

Both parties being married is another pattern, but I don't have a clue how the pieces fit together. No sickness checks for a wedding band before the infection sets in, and even with a fifty-fifty divorce rate, people who break up don't *literally* eat each other alive. It could be coincidence, but it sure as hell doesn't feel that way.

Not with that stain in the sink. What are the odds two completely different people drag a bloody hand up and over to a drain, then die on the floor a few feet away? Falling isn't the cause—the smear goes in the wrong direction.

If I didn't know any better, I'd say something climbed out and escaped. Maybe that's what I was seeing at the scene outside earlier; a trail through the pipes, slipping from one apartment to another. I do a quick search on my phone for info on parasites, looking for any kind of illness or vermin that could breed so big in a person's body. The lack of such an explanation—denial by omission—should be comforting, but I'm left with a gut-wrenching question.

If you were starving, if you were scared, if a monster was inside someone you loved, wouldn't you do anything to get it out? I've been there before, trying to bleed the beast and having it come back twice the size, hooked on you and hungry.

"Shit," I mutter. "I can't tell if I'm brilliant or I've finally lost my goddamn mind."

Talking to myself in the middle of a crime scene isn't filling in a lot of points on the first column. Any claim I make needs proof, in case the cops come and sweep everything away. Enough blood lingers in the drain for me to scrape a chunk into a new vial without disturbing anything else, although I don't dare take a taste this time.

Not what after grew out of the first sample.

The hour is too late—well, too early—to text Nikki and let her know what I'm thinking. She probably won't believe a damn word, but it's the only idea I have. Anything that can kill like this and get away untouched is a danger to everyone.

Question is, who's next on the chopping block?

SIX

I WAKE UP TO my third alarm going off, and a cascade of blood pouring down my sleep shirt in a sticky, clotting flood.

The shirt is done for, so I pull the whole thing off and ball the fabric up, pinching under the bridge of my nose with my other hand to stem the tide. I could just suck it back under my skin like a sponge, but the sensation freaks me out. Blood might dance when I play a tune, but I've got no plans to be a career musician.

And using this horrible excuse for a superpower to play janitor feels like cheating. Years of obliterating my nasal passages with a cartel's worth of coke has consequences. Making anyone—or any*thing*—clean up after my own mistakes is uncomfortable at best.

Especially when I could go for a line or two right now. Good blow makes you immortal, awake, a wolf with the sun between bold and grinning teeth. Sober, I'm an empty husk playing host to some cardiovascular creep that won't give me the dignity of an introduction. My hair is going gray ten years early, my memory has more holes in it than a Republican media presser, and my last clean shirt is a fast fashion massacre.

When my phone buzzes, I move to slap the alarm again, but it's a text from Nikki.

NIKKI

We're having a memorial for Scott and Patricia at 4 inside the co-op. Stop by?

If anyone else was asking, I'd swipe away the notification without a second thought. Crowds are a killer for me without hypnotic music and a good buzz to even out the edges of panic. I miss that world in the middle of the night, dancing and laughing with strangers who never asked my name. I found a space between the leather dykes and drag queens, welcomed on the notion that we overlapped somewhere. Unfortunately, the gap was a foot or so wide and six feet deep.

When half the people around you are dead queers walking, your view of the world skews. If survival isn't on the table, holding back is pointless. Why drink less, smoke less, go home early? Folks like Nikki are trying to make the world better, but until that night in the bathtub, I couldn't understand the reason. It's no wonder

I'm dating a woman seventy spiritual years my senior. Letting the world end is easier than fighting to live, every day of the week.

So being a better person means going to the memorial, even if I'd rather chop off my hands at the wrist.

A shower handles the blood and scours the heavy film of sleep off my mind. I sort through my closet for an outfit even vaguely suitable for a funeral, but the results are middling: a plain black T-shirt generic in its inoffensiveness, and a pair of jeans without holes. My boots spent three hours soaking last night, so at least they're clean.

The memorial is only an hour away, but I text Nikki back to keep myself accountable.

CAMERON

I'll be there. Should I bring anything?

Her reply is instant.

NIKKI

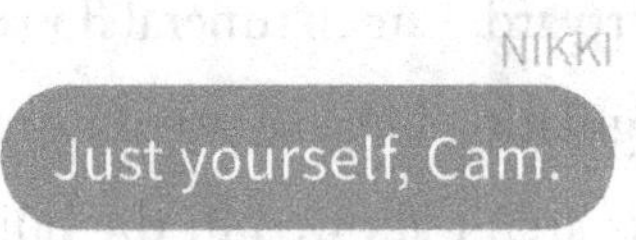

I could walk down to the cemetery and burn time away with Katherine, but daylight complicates things. She can't leave her grave without a body to anchor to, and bleeding on a headstone with groundskeepers and the grief-stricken public walking around is asking to be arrested for disturbing the peace.

Luckily, they let me off with a ticket the first time, but Kat warned me not to do it again. With the way this week is going, the cops prowling around the neighborhood will be trying to cover their asses, and I'm more likely to get a bullet than a write-up.

I flip through the news on my phone, hunting for public acknowledgement, but from a journalistic standpoint, the Norths and Hayes's don't seem to exist. Is a murder really a murder when the cops cart the bodies off and don't tell anyone? Even if I find whoever—or whatever—is doing this, the chain of evidence is screwed beyond repair. I can't exactly use my pulse reading trick to detect lies in a court of law.

Maybe Nikki won't mind if I show up early. If I have to be stuck alone in my own head for the next forty-five minutes without distraction, I might start drawing on the walls in blood without being asked to.

The co-op's front door is propped open, with a note taped to the frame inviting memorial attendees to head on through to the courtyard. I smell funeral flowers before I see them: a haze of roses coagulating like old perfume, undercut by the sweet tang of lilies. Cats aren't allowed in the building, but they wander the neighborhood at will. I'll have to remind Nikki when she throws the bouquets out; the whole co-op might snap from stress if poisoned animals start showing up on the street.

She's setting up foil trays of food with Tasha when I walk in. The collective of sun-bleached chairs are laddered on top of each other in the corner, ashtrays hiding underneath their layered legs. Enough space was squeezed out for the table, the flowers, and a blown-up picture of Scott and Patricia caught in a hug and smiling at each other. The resolution is terrible, something Nikki must have yanked off their socials, but it's not like they were up for a photo after the fact.

"You're early," Nikki says when she turns around, raising a brow. "That's pleasantly out of character."

"It's this new thing I'm trying," I joke. "You doing okay?"

"I'd be better if anyone at City Hall was answering my phone calls. They don't want a press release about the deaths, because investors are looking into the ward next door. Combo that with the police refusing to file a report, and I'm sunk."

Because who cares about the dead when there's cash to be pressed like wine out of the living. They would gentrify all of us into an early grave if they could. "Did you get the cremation money together?"

Nikki nods. "Everyone pitched in to help cover, and the Unitarians down the way gave us half their farmer's market sales. It was really sweet. I'm just worried about…"

"More," I finish for her. "This happening again."

Worry pulls a crease into Nikki's brow. "Do you have any idea what's going on, Cameron? I don't get spooked by much, but I knew Ellis and Ricardo. Their fundraiser brunches are half the reason I got voted in."

Now they're dead, and no one who cares can do anything that matters. "I found a connection between the two cases, but until I know what's killing them in the first place, there's not much I can do."

"But the same person did this?" she asks.

Nikki needs something to cling to. Hope doesn't do the trick for me, but if it makes her day any better, I'll offer a lie with my whole chest. "Yeah, looks that way."

"God. We've got cops killing kids every other month, but they can't catch a cannibal, or whoever the hell this is?" She shakes her head, sighs, and starts prying the thin, white cardboard lids off the food. "Folks are going to be here soon. Feel free to get a plate."

"Actually, there's something I wanted to show you. It's evidence, so don't freak out, but I wanted to make sure—"

I'm interrupted by the creak of the courtyard door. Two young women walk in, followed by a somber third. When they return my smile of welcome with awkward grimaces, my throat tightens. I must look how I feel: a walking stress fracture. Nikki is generous enough to ignore it, but a pack of grieving strangers have enough on their minds without entertaining my half-hearted attempts at socializing.

Better to go for the food. Tasha presides over the newly exposed mourning meal, forcing a smile when our eyes finally meet. We've never talked much; I think she considers me to be her wife's pet project more than a friend.

Nikki greets everyone—Danielle, Si Wei, Maz—inviting them to eat as the rest of the co-op pours in. I have no idea what's good, and Tasha's polite empty stare is making my neck itch, so I scoop a bit of everything onto one plate and vacate to the corner by the chairs. The tears and hugs have already started, which leaves me playing a critic in the front row of a theater, trying to understand the saddest interpretive dance I've ever seen.

I should have shown Nikki the vials and left. Now I'm going to be boxed in here listening to old potluck stories and co-op group chat memes until everyone crowds the buffet table to restore post-sobbing calories.

"Cameron?" Nikki's voice snaps me away from the uncomfortable spectacle of the mourners. "You okay?"

"Feeling a little out of place," I admit.

"I was talking about the food. You wolfed down half of it like you've never eaten before."

She gestures at my grease-logged paper plate, and I look down. It's a conglomerate mush of potatoes and vegetables, pockmarked with nuggets of fried chicken and shredded beef, half-drowned in viscous gravy. The huge gouge in the center must be courtesy of my fork, but I didn't taste a thing. My gut churns, caught between knife-like pangs and the queasy strain of eating too much in too few bites.

"Appetite's been kind of off lately." The fact that I'm eating anything is amazing, considering what I keep walking in on. "Do you care if I go? This... I shouldn't be here, Nikki. I don't know these people."

The concern on her face fades to sympathy, which cuts twice as deep. "You could get to know them. I worry about you living alone, Cam."

Because at the end of the day, Nikki can't see anything but an addict. Not wrong, I guess, but in terms of trouble, my past habits are the tip of the iceberg. "I'm good. Can you look at something for me real quick? Then I'm getting out of here."

Her answer is a reluctant nod, so I put my plate down on top of the chairs and pull out the vials. I expect the blood, the stringy webs of mold—what I don't expect is the samples pressed flat against the sides of the glass like two magnets trying to snap together. They twitch between my fingers, and I almost drop them both.

"Fuck!" Clutching the vials to my chest is a quick save, but the people gathered in the courtyard turn at the sound. That many eyes on me at once makes every vein in my body caustic with heat, burning its way up the back of my skull into a single demand: *Look away!*

"I need to go."

"Cameron, what is that?" Nikki asks, frowning. "What are you holding?"

I can't show her. They're moving of their own accord, which means using my own brand of weird bullshit to figure out the reason, far away from here. "Evidence I took from the scenes. Just keep people out of the Hayes's room, okay? And don't go to the North's's apartment either."

Her frown deepens. "I wasn't going to. Explain what's going on so I can help you."

Nikki cares about me, but I'm not equipped to handle this emotional ping-pong and solve what's killing people at the same damn time. My brain scatters at a moment's notice on a good day; under pressure, it's liable to give up the ghost entirely. "I'll tell you when I have the truth."

Shoving the vials back in my pocket and zipping it tight, I push past her and leave the courtyard without a word. For once the social contract saves me: Nikki would never abandon half a dozen people alone at the memorial she personally organized. Once I'm outside the co-op, I slip into the maze of alleys between our buildings, and take the vials out again.

I wasn't seeing things. The samples are the color of mud now, completely pierced through by stringy brown growth. Every thread strains against the glass, trying to reach their twins in the other vial. The tremble is subtle, but getting stronger.

"Attracted to your own kind, huh?" I mutter. "You and me both, buddy."

I can use this. Fuck, I can *use* this.

Pulling the vials apart takes more effort than I expect, but blood is blood, deteriorated or not. Drawing on my own sends a rush of heat to my palms, seeping through the glass to make a connection.

A pull answers like a fist around my heart. It's like the link I sensed between the North and Hayes's houses, but stronger. I stumble a few steps forward before steadying out, rust-colored spots corroding the edge of my vision, but a sudden sense of where they're trying to go rolls through me, inexorable as gravity. Shoving one vial in each pocket to keep them separate, I move by feel instead of sight, hooking between narrow canals of dumpsters and worn brick until I'm standing in front of the train station.

Good thing I brought my transit card.

The pull takes me to the northbound tracks, where a train has just rolled in. This one is swathed in red, white, and blue, although the message painted on the side is more practical than patriotic: THE RED LINE IS NOW THE BLOOD LINE. Underneath little drops imitating sanguine tears, the byline declares *Help Get Chicago's Blood Supply on Track*. A laugh leaves my lips before I can stop it.

"I'm doing my best," I mumble to the car before stepping on board. "Keeping the neighbors intact is hard work."

Two kills made this thing strong enough to crawl a block; four seems to have given it free rein to move into a whole new neighborhood, fresh territory. I don't really want to think about what kind of intellect that implies, a sickness using human strategies to avoid getting caught.

My shoulder bumps another, and I tighten my grip around the vials to keep them safe. A man melting out of his Cubs shirt sneers at me, holding the rail high enough to expose the entire car to his beer sweat, fresh from the stadium.

"Watch where you're going, faggot."

"Call me that again and I'll pop your eyes like balloons, asshole," I spit.

He stares at me, stunned that I dared to respond. With the week I've had, he's lucky I'm content with the threat. When I smile, his watery blue gaze darts away from mine, followed by a low grunt of "Freak."

Arguing that would be a waste of energy. I move down a car but stay by the doors, waiting for the tremors between my fingers to drag in a different direction. Two stops later, the vials convulse. Both hands are blood-stiff, hypersensitive. I don't usually keep myself under this long, but considering the work this personal nightmare machine puts me through, it had better keep up its end of the bargain.

My body is twitching like a Geiger counter on the way down the station stairs and back to the street. The world is overlaid with a crimson stain, as if a dark room filter flipped in my brain, color-blind in reverse. I'm walking toward a knot of plaque in the city's arteries, squeezed narrow and necrotic. A car almost hits me when

I mistake the light at the crosswalk, but any Chicago driver worth their winter salt knows to expect pedestrians scurrying across the streets with no sense of self-preservation. Right now, I'd make a lab rat look mindful.

Granville Street leads past a host of gyms and juice bars to a quiet block of apartments with grown-over wooden fences. One of them is missing enough slats for me to step through, emerging in a parking lot cobbled together from spilled gravel and white paint, lines knocked askew. The back door doesn't have a lock so much as a spring coiled in tight hostility, ready to pop like shrapnel the moment the frame jiggles too hard. Yet it lets me pass without incident, closing with an ear-piercing creak.

Something solid slams into the floor right above my head, followed by a scream. An elevator cuts open the end of the hall, but hell if I'm trusting machinery from the Powell era. I take the stairs two at a time and shove my way through the door onto the next floor.

The screaming has stopped, but at the edge of my hearing are choked, heaving sobs—from the second apartment on the left. When I step past the threshold, no one's in sight, but the coat closet is the source of the sound. Praying I'm not about to get my face chewed off, I turn the knob and yank the door open.

"Please God, no—" The woman curled up on the floor pleads, arms wrapped around herself in a desperate shield. Blood soaks her shirt, ragged holes torn open across her stomach and ribs. "Please, Mike, don't—"

"I'm not Mike," I whisper, trying to break the fugue of sheer terror. "What's happening? Where is he?"

A violent retching sound answers for her. I whip around as a tall, heavyset man stumbles out of the bathroom. Scratches mar his face, mouth and chin coated with sticky yellow bile. Gray eyes widen and roll until nothing shows but the whites, his jaw going slack as a broken hinge. It clicks and jerks as he tries to swallow around the massive bulge distorting his throat, flesh stretched to its limit by something thrashing deep inside.

Skin splits with a slick, visceral tear, and a writhing mass of blood and tendrils lunges at my chest.

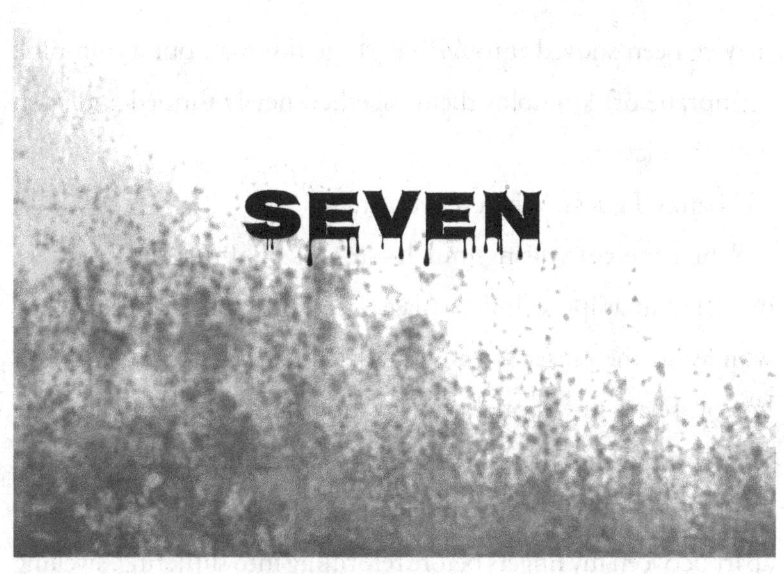

SEVEN

I'VE ALWAYS BEEN TERRIBLE at sports.

Which might be why my reaction to a bizarre, softball-sized morass going for my heart is to slap it between both hands rather than a proper catch. Gore-soaked cirri infiltrate my knuckles, burying into tendons and bone, but drawing blood is its first mistake. My flesh fuses back together, shoving the razor-sharp tips out with a raw squelch. Finding a grip, I throw the writhing bundle at the wall with every bit of desperate burnout strength in me. It hits with a grotesque slap, sending gobbets of Mike's flesh flying across the kitchen.

Mike himself is done for, collapsed on the floor. His eyes bulge wide enough to strain the sockets, staring at the unwound remnants of his carotid artery. The amount of blood around him is a real slipping hazard, but blood is fuel. My hands hurt like they've been shoved through a garbage disposal, but a thin pink membrane of skin holds them together, newly formed and flush with circulation.

Thanks, I guess. Whatever you are.

When the convulsing mulch—it looks like a plant dyed red, drowned in adipose and cartilage—rears back to leap again, the woman in the closet screams again, impaled between grief and horror. I have just enough time to shove the door shut before the hungry bastard wraps tight around my arm, clinging like duct tape. Pulling at it is like trying to get a grip on rotten spaghetti, breaking apart between my fingers before reforming into slithering, swelling mush.

Monster Mash isn't the smartest thing in the world. My jacket stymies its brutal attempts to dig back under my skin as tendrils slide around, looking for an opening. So maybe this thing can't see—it senses heat, senses flesh.

Slamming my forearm into the door is a bad call, sending pain shooting up my shoulder. The rubbery mass seizes my wrist, trying to wrench the joint back, and over the pervasive reek of blood and decay, I smell smoke. The char is toxic, like plastic melting, and the second I spare to look at the kitchen reveals a crooked pot on the red-hot stove, billowing out wisps of black and gray as the handle loses its shape.

A stupid plan comes to mind, but stupid is what I've got. I stumble into the kitchen and seize the handle, agony searing down to the nerve as blisters bloom across my palm. The second the pot is out of the way, I slam the moldy motherfucker holding my other arm right into the glowing burner underneath.

It pops and crackles like dry wood thrown into a blazing bonfire. Frantic, seizing coils try to keep hold of my arm, but self-preservation wins out. Once the last miserable thread lets go of me, I turn the pot upside-down, dumping boiling hot water onto the bulk of its body. Enough scalding steam to rival an autoclave bursts to life on contact, but for good measure, I bring the scorched belly of the pot down hard, crushing the creature between the stove and sizzling stainless steel. Once—twice—three times.

As the cloud around the stove clears, the constant pump of adrenaline holding me up takes a nosedive. Dizzy and panting for breath, I stare at the charred mess smeared across the burner. The only hint of movement is faint wisps of smoke floating through its body. Keeping a wary hold on the pot, I flip the temperature knob to zero. Last thing anyone needs is this thing going up in flames and burning the damn apartment down.

I think—*I fucking hope*—it's dead.

Everything aches. My arms, my back, my skull, pain crashing over me in one wave after the next. The burns on my palm are in much better shape than they should be, but staring at a wealth of weeping blisters threatens even my gag reflex. Breathing deep helps, a little. I turn on the sink and shove both hands under the cold faucet, trying to rinse off the mess and give my obliterated nerves some relief.

By the time I turn the water off, a hindbrain's worth of sheer, convulsive panic has subsided, leaving me with a halo of a headache. Or maybe it's the high-pitched wails of despair filling with the apartment with a wall of noise.

Shit. The closet.

I step over Mike's corpse and tug the door open. The woman inside is curled up in a sobbing ball, rocking herself back and forth. When I kneel down in front of her, she flinches, caught in the raw paralysis of *please don't please don't*.

"It's over," I say, soft as I can. "You're okay."

The biggest goddamn lie in the world, of course, but telling the truth about what just happened sure as hell isn't going to make her feel any better.

My words sink in slow, but after another minute of staggered pleading, she looks up from the refuge of her arms. Tears and sweat soak her face, jaw so tight with fear that muscle bulges out from round cheeks.

"Mike," she gasps, "I'm so sorry, Mike."

"There was nothing you could do." The fact that I could do anything myself was blind, hysterical luck. "Can you tell me your name?"

She roughly wipes some of the damp mess away from dark brown eyes. "Jasmine."

For a second, I consider a fake name, but I think I blew out half my remaining brain cells trying to survive. Nothing good comes to mind. "Cameron."

Jasmine's eyes widen. "I know you. You work at the clinic."

Of course I do, but the question is how she knows this when I pull the night shift. "Sorry. My memory's shit."

"No, it's okay," she mumbles, "we never really met. I saw you at the HIV fundraiser."

Oh, right. They had me passing out flyers in return for some overtime pay. She must be a patient. "This visit isn't exactly on the books."

She accepts that with a tight nod. "Is... Is Mike dead?"

"Yeah. But so is the thing that was hurting him."

Jasmine's next sob borders on hysterical. "I thought it was me."

"What?"

"I thought I was hurting him. Or that he was going to hurt me. Mike was yelling, saying he was starving. He's never raised his voice to me before. I was trying to cook and I was so hungry too, but I never am, I—" She shakes her head, eyes brimming over with pain and confusion. "Mike touched me. Scratched me. And suddenly, I wanted to rip his throat open. The love of my life. I wanted to..."

Her words taper off, but the dread on Jasmine's face says volumes.

"You wanted to what?" I ask.

Nausea makes her confession thick with bile. "I wanted to eat him alive."

Oh. Everyone *has* been tearing each other apart, but that throat-bursting infestation is what's responsible. "How about now?"

"No! God, why would I ever—" Jasmine squeezes her eyes shut, new tears springing forth. "I loved him so much. What do I do?"

Calling the police is out of the question. At best, they would arrest us both. Examining Mike's body is pointless when I already know what killed him. What Jasmine needs is to get out of here, and what I need is to make sure every particle of this souped-up parasite gets sterilized off the face of the earth.

Searching my pockets turns up a card for a local women's shelter, which I offer to her with care. "Go wash your face and get changed. Take whatever you need from here, and ask for a room at this place. They'll let you in, no questions asked."

"But this is our apartment. Mike..."

"He was sick, Jasmine." I don't know what else to call it. "The city finds out about this, they're going to either send the CDC or CPD, but either way you're not going to want to be here when it happens. I'll get everything cleaned up, okay?"

She takes the card, smoothing her thumb over the clean black font. "Th-thanks."

I back away from the closet so Jasmine can unfold herself and stumble past the door. The wounded sound that leaves her at the sight of Mike dead on the floor echoes in my head, haunted and helpless. When she disappears into the bedroom, I return to the kitchen, hunting through drawers until I find a plastic bag with a zip-top.

Using a spatula to scrape off dead, charred, carnivorous mold from a stove might qualify as the worst cleaning job I've ever had. I gather every last blackened bit into the bag, press the air out, and seal it shut. The walls and floor need a formal introduction to industrial bleach, but thankfully the remaining mess is courtesy of Mike, rather than his parasitic passenger. His blood isn't what I'm worried will spread.

When I check the vials in my pocket, they're dry and still. Connecting to the pull again tells me the same thing—the trail stops right where I'm standing.

So I hide my surreal trophy in three layers of grocery bags, each one tied tight to make sure nothing slips out. Once I'm out of here, my next stop is the pet cremation place on Elston to dump the remains into their furnace. The operator there owes me for 'borrowing' half my club stash two years back after someone else spiked my drink. Turns out combining Rohypnol and LSD makes fever dreams look friendly.

Jasmine comes back out of her room, empty-eyed with grief. "Could you do me a favor?"

"Sure."

"My meds are in the kitchen." She gestures past Mike to a cabinet. "I can't walk over him, I can't—"

"It's fine," I say softly, "I'll get them."

He's just a body to me, but I'm careful not to step on anything still attached. Jasmine's pills crowd the entire bottom shelf of the cabinet, but the bottles are standard fare, anti-retrovirals and half a dozen assistants to aid the side effects. I couldn't get high on anything here if I tried.

The megestrol catches my eye for different reasons. If you're HIV positive, it's one of the best appetite stimulators to take. That's what Jasmine meant about not getting hungry—without the meds in her system, nausea would overwhelm everything else.

Is that what stopped her from killing Mike? What does this mold shit do to people?

I don't have answers, but Jasmine needs to get out of here before one of her neighbors decides to get brave and call the cops. She lets me escort her down the stairs—surprise, the elevator doesn't even work—and out to her car. Jasmine probably shouldn't be driving, but I never earned my license. The further away she is from here, the better.

"The last thing I said to him was so cruel," she whispers while starting up the engine. "I had never felt that angry before. We were struggling, but we always made it work. Why... How did I forget that?"

Whatever clawed out of Mike probably had the answer, but I can't interrogate ashes. "Don't worry about that right now. Get somewhere safe."

"Nowhere's safe," Jasmine mutters. "Not for us."

She looks over one shoulder to back out of the lot. After Jasmine's car disappears down the street, I slog my way onto the opposite block. It feels like I went six rounds with a wood chipper, but lying down is out of the question until business is taken care of at the crematorium.

All Paws Go to Heaven is a soft pastel pastiche of a waiting room and pet museum, where brass statues of beloved poodles and clay cat feet cost about twice as much as an actual human funeral. A cavalcade of acrylic animal eyes go full panopticon at me as I walk up to the antacid pink counter to find Neil.

He looks more put together than usual, but Neil is a night high kind of guy—the notorious 'functioning' addict who appears sober enough by daylight to escape suspicion. In practice, the hours don't matter when you're passed out on the floor on enough dope to drop a horse, but people like to pretend those on the fringes of society walk around with a spotlight over their heads, open for scorn or misplaced paternalism.

"Cameron." Blonde eyebrows shoot up towards his thinning hairline. "I haven't seen you in months. Looking good."

Liar. "As opposed to what? Dead?"

"I mean, you stopped showing up after Tommy kicked the bucket. Supply was so low for a while, I thought detox might have gotten you." Neil flinches into a smile. "Arnie went out that way, you know."

Anger crawls up the inside of my chest, squeezing around my heart. I *do* know that first name, clinging to a scrap of memory. "Tommy was a piece of shit. Everything he sold was either watered down or cut with fucking meth."

"Dealers, right?" He laughs, but the sound breaks into a wheezing cough. "What are you doing here, anyway?"

I hold up the layered plastic bag. Nothing inside has moved since I left Jasmine's apartment, but I'm not taking any risks. "You're going to burn this for me. Down to ash. Absolutely nothing left. Got it?"

"Cam, I can't do that." Neil scratches behind one ear, hard enough to leave flecks of red under his nails. "There's policy, you know. What's if that's a person or something?"

I raise a brow. "You're telling me you think a human being could fit in a bag this size?"

"Well, no, that's dumb. I just—" He crosses both arms, trying to puff out his chest. It would work better if Neil wasn't bird-thin, sallow angles jutting out from his arms and face. Heroin chic, my ass. "I don't want to lose my job."

"Then fork over the five hundred you owe me." I gesture to one of the brass statues, an overbred bulldog with more jaw than cranium. "You sell a couple of these a day, right? Should be easy to pay up."

"I…" Neil's laugh dies down faster this time. "Come on, Cameron. It's been ages."

"Yeah?" Leaning over the counter, I drop the bag right in front of him. It lands with a squish; he winces. "Doesn't that mean I should be collecting interest?"

"Oh, come *on*." Bloodshot blue eyes turn, pleading. "We used to have a lot of fun together. Why don't you wait until I'm off work, then I'll hook you up with something nice?"

With Neil, 'nice' is contextual. The goods are always borrowed from someone else he owes. Back in the day, that wouldn't have bothered me, but even the best product in the world can't touch me now. More's the pity. "Burn it or pay up."

"Fine. Jesus Christ." Neil picks up the bag by the top loop, holding it away from his body like radioactive waste. Honestly, the thing I killed is probably worse. "You're mean as hell without something cooling you off."

"Yeah. Can only imagine why."

"Spare me the sob story," he sneers. "We've all got problems."

I let him storm off into the back without another word. What's there to say? He and I were never friends, only the living embodiment of misery loving company. If I'm not self-destructing, we have nothing in common. I let a lot of people hurt me—and hurt them in return—because sharing a needle masqueraded as compassion. Shocking that any of us are left, when those who have the chance at freedom get poisoned on the way out.

The furnace makes a horrible sound when it heats up, a low and piercing vibration. Neil's order of operations seems to be cursing every step of the way, his machine-gun-quick swearing undercut by the click of dials and switches. When I hear the rustle of plastic and a slow tear, I nearly throw myself over the counter.

"Don't you fucking open that," I snap. "Mind your business."

"I'm not supposed to put stuff like this in the fire!" Nonetheless, the rustling stops. "It's bad for the environment."

"Yeah, and ecstasy production kills a million trees in Cambodia a year, so hop off the high horse, okay?"

"What?" Neil actually sounds surprised. "That sucks."

It's no different than anything else. We've razed half the planet for profit as much as pleasure, and everything we eat and own is built off the backs of other people. One nihilistic existential crisis too many is part of why my drug use went from recreational to compulsory—I wanted to feel good before the end came. Maybe somebody else would solve the big problems, and I'd wake up in a brighter world. If not, I'd die with a smile on my face.

Oblivion looks a lot like bliss if you stack your bets the right way.

Neil emerges twenty minutes later, soaked with sweat and peeling off a set of ash-choked gloves. "There, I burned your garbage. Happy?"

"Overjoyed." I'm fucking exhausted. Destroying that thing is worth a nap, I think. "See you later, Neil."

"Don't count on it," he mutters.

The Red Line is close, so I can catch a train and get some shuteye before clocking in for work. I should probably shower too, if only because bits of Mike ended up on my pants and shoes. Nobody on the street seems to notice, but that's one of my favorite things about this city—we prefer to stay out of each other's business. Don't start none, won't be none, as wiser people than I have said.

Except there's one person who needs to know what I've been up to. I text Nikki while heading up the stairs

CAMERON

Sorry for ducking out early, but I found out what hurt everyone.

Little gray dots bounce across my screen before she answers.

NIKKI

You did? Are you okay? What happened?

CAMERON

Doesn't matter. It's dead.

NIKKI

Was it an animal? Cam, you have to tell me.

Lucky for her, I don't.

Instead, I lock the door behind me and strip. Everything needs to go in the washing machine, but that's a problem for future Cameron. After turning my phone to silent and tossing it on the charger, I climb onto ice cold sheets, hoping beyond hope that I'm too worn out to dream.

EIGHT

THE NEXT DAY, I'M running on autopilot.

My head is heavy as a stone, my throat is dry, and I'm starving. Call it a crossfaded hangover, except for once, I haven't done anything to earn the consequences. Isn't saving a woman's life worth a get-out-of-jail free card for migraines? The job-well-done high lasted less than five minutes.

Frost is sticking to the windows, so I throw on a robe and pants before heading to the kitchen. Making coffee is a comedy of errors, except I'm not laughing by the time I've spilled the beans trying to get them in the grinder for the third time. The damn burrs barely want to turn as is, and the staticky click each time I try warns me that some bit of machinery inside is one wrong tap away from breaking. I shove it across the counter, then look down at my hands.

Despite being split open to the bone yesterday, everything seems to be in order. I flex each finger one at a time, rub my palms together, and make tight fists, waiting for a twinge or other red flag. Normal as flesh can be, considering what's lurking underneath. You would think anything capable of healing brutal injury could handle first grade motor function.

"Why don't you fix my fucking brain while you're at it?" I growl.

No answer, of course. Even looking at the grinder is pissing me off, so I give up and head into the bathroom to shower. By habit, I hit the light switch. The tub is clean and white as acid-bleached bone, reflecting with a gleam that makes my eyes contract. When I try to slap the light off again, I miss.

Son of a—

A message is written in blood on the mirror, every letter stark and hours dry: **I CAN'T GET IT OUT.**

Get *what* out?

My eyes snap to the glass, body wrenched parallel. I've got a Cassius sort of look going on, lean enough for it to show in the hollows of my cheeks. Keeping my hair short is more for convenience than any real sense of aesthetic, but it darts every which way, spiked like someone ran grease-damp hands through it. My teeth have held together, one bit of genetic luck amidst everything else, blunt and imperfect.

"What are you?"

My face is moving, but the words aren't mine. I didn't say a thing.

Blinking and biting my tongue doesn't clear the hallucination. Staring at the stained reflection in the mirror offers no answers either, only the subtle widening of pupils, like the aperture of a camera.

"What are *you*?" I ask.

A voice like a record scratch answers. Every syllable is a needle scraping bone inside my skull, piercing out through both ears and twisting furiously. "I'm looking good, killer. You were a hard nut to crack, but I finally got a good grip. See?"

My jaw goes slack, tongue lolling out. In the back of my throat, rust-colored threads pulse, damp with mucus. They overlay every vein like a shadow, roots without anchor, thick enough to make me gag.

Except I can't. My throat is in the grip of an invisible hand, holding me in place until my teeth suddenly knock together.

"Fuck you—" Speech is mine again, but only for a second. My eyelids get yanked open and shut, blinking so many times I go dizzy. Gripping at the sink is only half a success; one hand claws at the rounded edge, the other stays rubbery and slack.

"Answer me." The scratch returns, working scalpel-sharp around my temples. "What's inside you, huh? The rest of your kind don't even know I'm here."

"Good question," I choke out. "Never figured that one out."

"Don't play me, Cameron."

My throat collapses on itself, cutting off any hope of air. The breath in my lungs is trapped, turning carbon toxic with nowhere else to go. White and red flashes at the edges of my vision like sirens, acting just as goddamn useless.

Blood rushes up from panicked lungs, a hot and violent sting. I start coughing it all over the sink, splattering red backwash up to the marred mirror, but I can breathe. The visceral overload subsides after a few more hacking coughs, and I can move both of my hands again. Small mercies.

"I wasn't playing you, jackass," I hiss through stained teeth. "Whatever just kicked you around works on its own schedule."

"Liar!" It snarls, coiling and sharp, clawing at the underside of my scalp. "I've felt you use that power. I saw you draw on the walls. Watched you snake through blood to find a trail. You found my brother, and you *burned* him."

Him. Of course. Trying to worm back under my flesh like a parasite after a lifetime of return to sender. I might have snorted half my cognitive capacity to powder over the years, and that's on me, but so many pieces fall together at once that all I can do is stare mindlessly in the mirror. At least the blood tried to leave behind a warning. "Huh?"

A poisonous rebuke flenses my nerves and hangs them out to dry. When I'm done twitching, it snaps, "You heard me."

Well, yeah. If this thing saw me painting in blood, it's been inside me for days, since the night I set foot in the Hayes's apartment. "I had you, right at the start. You shocked my tongue like a fork in an electric socket."

"I was a couple aborted cells left from my twin's birth," it—he—counters, words dripping with oily amusement. "Wouldn't have gone anywhere if you hadn't taken a taste. We're born like a bee sting, leaving behind the guts to go somewhere new."

I'm too distracted by the notion that this parasite might have hostile sentience to immediately answer. When the truth sinks in, I have to laugh. "Joke's on me."

"Would have been funny if it hadn't led you to him." A wry scoff wrenches itself past my throat. "You weren't supposed to see me. You weren't supposed to see *us*."

So it goes both ways. This talkative monstrosity set up shop in my skin, but he can't hide any more than I can. "My condolences."

The sarcasm earns me a second attempted throttling, but before my throat can snap shut again, blood answers. I don't particularly enjoy gagging on my own fluids, but if that's the price of oxygen, I'll deal.

Whatever this growth is, he's in deep. Since my primary passenger has yet to spit him out à la cheap tobacco, the only tool left in my kit is everything the kindly folks at Xanthous taught me about conflict resolution. Step one: identify the problem.

"You got a name?" I ask.

"No," he uses my tongue, savoring the denial like a piece of candy. "Give me one."

I snort. "You don't want me making that decision. Take my word for it."

Pressure seizes my eyes, lips drawn back in a tight rictus as he tugs my face around like a Halloween mask, stretching until flesh strains like rubber. "I said *give me one*."

Motherfucker, that hurts. "Fine. You're Leech. How about that?"

A wet, delighted wheeze echoes between my ears. "I'm the Leech, yeah. I like that word. Scott was screaming it at Patricia once I got him. Your local news *loves* it. Leech, Leech, Leech!"

How the hell does this slab of moss know so much? Good thing step two is 'get context'. "Pretty smart for a couple of dumpstered cells."

"I'm everything my brother was. Lead, asbestos, black mold. They built high streets in this neighborhood to keep the cholera out. Not down south, though. Fertile territory." Leech croons, continuing to work the inside of my head like a turn table. "But I'm uptown now, baby! I would have been alone, left to rot, if not for you."

Because I gave him a new terrarium. "You're welcome."

"Welcome for what, you fucking stain?! I'm the future, the new ooze, the sickness that was always coming. Your kind incubated me for decades and have the nerve to resist?" His anger pours like boiling oil into my skull, sizzling until there's nothing left but a cooked, quivering hunk of meat. "You. Killed. Him."

Despite the pain, I can't help but smile. "So you're the only one left?"

Leech quiets, but the rage simmering in my gray matter says plenty.

"Doesn't matter." He steals my mouth for the answer, chaining my eyes to every subtle movement in the mirror. "Only thing stopping me from making you a full-time figurehead is that pesky barrier between blood and brain."

"Why bother?" I ask. "Your so-called brother punched his way out of three throats in a row. If you're going to kill me, get it over with."

"No, no, Cameron!" Leech says, saw-like and sing-song, "I'm tired of the small fry. Making them cry and beg as they claw open my cocoon. I don't want new wings. I want a home where I can feast to bursting."

The only good thing about living with suicidal ideation on the back burner is the notion that I would rather die isn't as stressful as it could be. "So that's why you went after couples. You can get in someone, but you can't get out by yourself."

"Used to be we could." He chuckles; a thread of bloody spittle drips down my chin. "But every time we eat one of you, we get bigger. Spent months in that first body, growing and listening. Learning what makes your kind tick."

"Who was your first? Scott?"

"That sad sack? Not a chance. He was just my taxi to the North Side. I jumped him after he almost buzzed me in half."

The fucking pipes. Scott didn't just steal copper, he was the personal chauffeur to the monster tearing up the neighborhood. First in the mouth, then out through the sinks. Which begs another—and far worse—question.

"How many people did you kill in the South Side?"

"Lots." Leech gargles out another laugh. "Kept expecting to get caught. But I heard about the cops a *long* time before I ever saw one in the flesh. Wish I could have tried a pig on for size before finding you."

They did this. If a single goddamn detective had paid attention to people dying in a poor Black neighborhood, this vampiric Chia Pet wouldn't be up my ass. How many bodies did they ignore, never write reports for? Every member of so-called law enforcement would be better off littering the bottom of Lake Michigan.

"Oh, that riled you, did it?" Leech drawls. "Felt that in your stomach, in your spine. Felt it when those big men dragged you around that crime scene like a puppet. But you *are* a puppet, Cameron. Only thing that changes is who gets to hold your strings."

He's not wrong. I have been for most of my life, either to drugs and dealers or the thing swimming in my blood. Helping people around the neighborhood, helping Nikki make things better, was only my piece of independence, proof I could do more than being led around by the nose. Life is so much easier when someone else calls the shots, when their demands drown out my broken goddamn brain.

Unfortunately for Leech, the hard road is looking awful welcoming right now.

"Oh, yeah? Because I'll bleed myself dry if that means starving you out of existence. If that doesn't work, I'll stay in here until dehydration does me in. You can rot inside this puppet until the end finally comes for you. No new body. No way out."

"I don't need your *higher functions* to get what I want, Cameron." The threads in my throat wind into a braid, then slip down. Much farther down. "Your thoughts and memories? That's just gravy. Your blood? It'll give up when you do. But I squeeze the right gland like a sponge, well..."

Agony is an imperfect word. Human language never drummed up the right syllables to encompass the sudden flood of acid in my nerves, trying to eat themselves and everything in close proximity. I'm distantly aware of being on the floor, but nothing else parses until the pain leaves, swift as it arrived.

"Hurts, huh?" Leech asks, undeniably rhetorical. "Doesn't have to be this way. I *want* you with me. It can feel good, if you cooperate."

Trying to talk is hard when my tongue is swollen—I must have bitten it—and the inside of my throat feels like freshly poured concrete. Staying on the floor sounds like a much better way to spend my energy, so I lay there until Leech starts muttering again.

"What the fuck is wrong with you?" he demands.

I wouldn't even know where to start. "Want that list chronological or alphabetized?"

"You should be high as hell right now. Oxytocin, dopamine, serotonin. You've got more pumping through those veins than a Roman orgy."

Damn, that's funny. I laugh, even though it stings, because I'm not sure what else to do with Leech pulling every chemical lever in my body like a slot machine. Too bad this one was rigged from the start.

He yanks my jaw shut. "Stop making noise and explain. Now."

One upside of addiction is that it gives you an honorary minor in biochemistry. "Even if I hadn't fried half the receptors in my brain OD'ing, my sanguine friend is real strait-laced. No full body highs for me, Leech. Not anymore."

"Think that's going to stop me?" I'm forced back to stand in a few jerky, unsettling movements. He might have slithered through my muscles, but Leech isn't as experienced in using them. Good to know. "I don't need a carrot. Happy to use the stick until you behave."

"That would be a lot more believable if you didn't phrase things like a first time daddy dom," I say, braced for the pain to come.

Bracing doesn't do shit. To my credit, I end up huddled over the sink choking on my own snot and tears this time. Better than the floor, better than giving in to Leech's watered-down Milgram routine.

Eventually, it stops, if only so he can hear himself talk again. "You don't care about yourself? Fine. Easy fix."

Leech puppets my hand like it's made out of stone, but that doesn't stop him from reaching into the pocket of my robe. He pulls out my phone and holds it up to the light, getting a feel for the shape. When my thumb is dragged across the screen to wake it up, Nikki's last text is sitting there, still waiting for a reply.

Fuck.

"You like her, don't you?" Leech says, bright with glee. "And she's the one who sent you after me, isn't she?"

"Who cares?" I grind out.

"Well I do, Cameron. Because I'm going to call her over here, and the second she comes in, I'm going to eat her alive. You're going to watch and feel every second of it. How she bleeds, how she begs for you to stop. Until there's nothing left."

I smash the phone into the sink. It's the violence of reflex, hitting at a poor angle, but once I start, stopping is impossible. The screen shatters against the steel faucet, and the next time I bring it down, shards of plastic fly everywhere. He manages to yank my hand back once, but I put my entire body into the next swing, driving my clenched fist into the mirror.

The surface cracks in a crystalline spiral. Raw impact splinters down to the bone, jagged pieces jutting from my hand like brass knuckles, but better that than watching this motherfucker contort my face. Broken bits of my phone drop from weak fingers, little more than glue and a half-dead battery.

"Now look what you did," Leech hisses, the last word ending on a cackle. "That's all on you, Cameron."

Yeah, yeah. Different day, same story.

When I try and pry the biggest piece out, he locks my limbs in place. I grimace, struggle, but the glass falls out of its own accord, pushed aside by flesh forcibly knitting itself back together. Thankfully, my phone can't regenerate.

"Good luck making calls now," I say.

"Think you're real smart, don't you?" Leech snaps, harsh as a femur split to the marrow. "Waste all the energy you like. It just lets me in faster."

Giving up my last few hours for Nikki is one of the easier choices I've ever had to make. Shame they can't always be like that.

"We could cooperate if you weren't so damn stubborn." He's speaking faster now, on a tear. "I just wanna eat. Everybody has to.

I can feed off anybody, someone you don't like so much. That man on the train. Those cops. Give me a name."

"Sorry, fresh out."

Leech throws me around the room like a cat in a sack. I hit the towel bar—that seems to be a favorite of his—and get the belly of the sink shoved in my gut before he forces my hand into the shining hole in the middle of the mirror. Serrated edges slice through the nailbeds, pierce into the sides of my palm, deep enough to feel, too shallow for my blood to force back out.

"Listen here, you junkie piece of trash. Either you can relax in the passenger seat or I can throw you in the trunk. Doesn't matter either way. Got it?"

I steal back just enough of my face to grin. "I think I'd rather crash the car."

What I need is the razor on the ledge. One long stroke across the thigh can bleed me out fast enough that even Blood 2.0, or whatever's in my system, won't be able to heal in time. The femoral artery sprays like a fire hose. Sure, it's a lethal solution, but I've already been hijacked like a 757. No making the jump if I completely lose control.

Katherine is bound to be upset, but maybe the coin of my soul will land right side up and let me join her. I wouldn't mind haunting Chicago with her for the next eternity, and well, if things land the other way—I won't be around to complain. Nikki might take it even harder, but at least the thing killing the people she cares about will be gone. One day, she'll feel better, and I'd rather gamble on that than the fragile thread connecting me to existence.

It's been a pretty good run, all things considered.

My veins burn white-hot as I push with everything I have, shoving Leech into the back seat so I can grab the razor. His roar of protest is the static of a radio between channels, a chorus of gut-shot angels singing me off. Yet the world spins as my fingers brush the wooden handle, as if every drop of blood in my body just left my head.

"Not looking so hot, Cam," Leech mocks, but even his awful, skull-grinding voice sounds a million miles away.

As I sag onto my knees, the world goes black.

NINE

FOUR COLD WHITE WALLS surround me like a cradle.

Trying to sit up sends me sliding back down, too weak to lever myself back to equilibrium. Good news: my hands are intact. Bad news: I'm still alive, and that sure as hell wasn't the plan.

What even happened? I've never been so dizzy in my life. If anything, my balance is surprisingly good, enough to pass field sobriety tests when cops yanked my drunk ass off the street on my way home. The blood was just—

Protecting itself. Stopping its host from certain death.

"We have bigger problems at hand!" I shout, staring at the cracked lines of the bathroom ceiling. Sure, the bastard is running through my veins, but I'm yelling at the world too, at God, at anything that might happen to be listening.

I'm yelling at the letters it must have ripped out of me before going under, splattering the wall in accusatory red:

YOU NEVER GAVE ME A NAME

True enough. People hold names for things they care about. Friends, enemies, partners—whether the draw comes from love or hate. Names are definitions and connections, wrapping up intimacy into a few crucial syllables, impossibly small but undeniably powerful.

If I named this thing in my veins, it would be admitting everything that happened to me since that night is real. Maybe going unconscious was a good thing. My own damn blood hates me, and Leech doesn't seem like he's going to be shutting up any time soon.

"Rise and shine, beautiful!"

Case in point.

Rhetorical victory is short-lived when I'm wrenched from sitting to standing, a bend of spine and muscle that I distinctly lack the flexibility for. Pain answers in a lick of hellfire down my back, balance askew as my feet twist against sweat-damp porcelain.

I collapse back against the tub in a tangle of limbs, panting for breath as adrenaline briefly outpaces the forces playing with my body for keeps. For half a second, I'm just some mindless animal, and it's pretty damn nice.

"Oop." Leech hacks up a laugh. "I almost got you. Just need to worm up into that cerebellum and adjust the steering a little bit."

I get that he's been stealing space in other people for a while now, but the fact that a hunk of rotten salad sounds so goddamn Midwestern is fucking with me. "How'd you figure out this shit out, anyway?"

"Television," he declares proudly. "The first one of you I ate never turned his off. He couldn't move much, on account of the bone cancer. Those tumors taught me as much as his tiny little screen."

Seriously? Let that not be literal. "Who was he?"

"Terrance something or other. When I first got big enough to climb out of the pipes, I found him, hooked up to an IV drip and staring at that screen. He could barely walk, could barely breathe. He had that window, and his daughter."

"So you ate him alive," I say.

"He was already being eaten! What does cancer do best? It *grows*, Cam. I learned how to sprout everywhere that I shouldn't be. Tear down the foundations, then spruce the place up for a new resident. Move in like it's the homeland, and plant my seeds. Orexin. Ghrelin. Catecholamines." Leech's pride swells like a blister under my tongue. "Learned those pretty words from his baby girl. She became a nurse, buried herself in debt, to take care of him."

The first two are appetite stimulants. Lots of the HIV positive patients at Xanthous take a dose when treatment evaporates any urge to eat.

Like Jasmine. That's why she didn't rip Mike apart. She could barely eat in the first place, needed the meds. Leech's brother could only do so much to push her broken buttons, the same way he can only push half of mine.

Catecholamines are old as evolution, from the first time something cornered us in the dark and we lashed out: it sparks fight-or-flight. Put them together and yeah, I see how you might eat another person. Even the one you share your life with.

People might write it off as mere chemicals, but I know better. The right mix can make anyone feel immortal enough to jump off a building in broad daylight, but a wrong one could convince the most mild-mannered nobody to start ripping out teeth.

"What was the nurse's name?"

Leech's gleeful laugh is a wet grind, like a chainsaw starting in mud. "Why do you care?"

Because everyone killed by this architect of horrors deserves to be remembered. "Professional curiosity."

"I'll tell you if..." He draws out the last word, warm and thick as taffy. "You tell me about your friend, Cameron. I want to know about Tommy."

Tommy with the goods. Tommy with the garish full-print shirts covered in saints and crucifixes. Tommy with his eyes blown out, surrounded by more drugs than I had ever seen in my life, boxing him in like a gilded reliquary.

What I say is, "Who?"

Leech's good humor evaporates as he pinches my orbital nerve until it screams. Well, I scream, watching the world drown in white until he deigns to let go. "You know who. I heard you with Neil. Hear you talking to yourself. You do that a lot, by the way. Never mind the dreams, thief of thieves. Be *honest* with me."

Maybe once the void in the middle of my vision goes away. "You can see my dreams?"

"I don't need to be deep in the good meat for that. Those pretty sparks dance on top, going every which way. Can't eat 'em, but at least they're entertaining."

"You already know the truth, then. Tommy was my dealer."

"*Was.* That's the operative word, isn't it? Hot knife cutting right to the heart of everything. Tell me, Cam. How did he die?"

"No idea." Sure, I could guess, but it's not like I looked into the details. "He was dead when I walked in."

Leech scoffs static into my skull. "Oh, yeah? Did you check his pulse?"

"His eyeballs were hanging down around his chin, so no."

"People can survive that," Leech says, like he wants to try the same thing out on me, "but you didn't call 911 either, did you?"

"Did I call an ambulance for my dealer?" Rage entangles my voice, weaving low and tight. "Did I let the cops know the person responsible for murdering a dozen of my friends had finally kicked the bucket? Did I want to help the absolute monster that cut a girl's coke with hookworm medication to make her fester from the inside out because she gave him a fake fifty? I don't fucking think so."

Tommy got away with it because he knew we couldn't afford anyone else. In the universal scheme of things, drugs aren't really the problem: money is. Most people don't kill for a couple of pills, they kill for the cash hiding behind them. He was more than happy to water down and poison his supply, because the good stuff was for people better than us. Why care if customers died sometimes? The cops wrote it off as victimless crime.

Maybe he was still breathing when I came in.

Maybe I didn't care.

And maybe I wanted him to watch me walk off with everything he worked for, knowing no one was coming to help.

"So noble. Choosing who lives and who dies." Leech clicks my tongue in distaste. "I bet you did the right thing, didn't you? Either tossed that junk out so it wouldn't hurt anyone, or gave your so-called friends the best free high of their lives. Right?"

Guilt chokes me better than Leech ever could.

"Do I have it wrong, Cameron?" He wiggles the needle of his words against the softest part of my ear, curling up in the drum. "Tell me."

"I took everything he had." Everything: bags of pills, stacks of blotter sheets, an entire brick of cocaine. Half of it I didn't even recognize, but you don't look for labels in an open bank vault, either. Tommy had promised me some hot new party drug; what I stole was a one way ticket to nirvana. "Carried it home in bags like groceries. Ran up the stairs laughing. Then started getting high."

I lost three days. I woke up drowning in blood. Maybe Tommy's new shit killed him, and maybe I mixed it with enough other shit to survive. Not that it really matters, because if we're comparing parasitic potency, Leech has me outmatched ten to one.

"Yeah, I thought so." Genuine sympathy invades his tone, which I don't like in the least. "That's why you need me."

"What?"

"When you were on your back in the black, I realized we've been going about this the wrong way. You and I could do so much together, Cameron."

Sure, I love Kool-Aid. Of course he'd offer me a cup. "How so?"

"You need a taste of good ambition. The juice! A whole apocalypse of power inside you, and what are you doing with it? Drawing symbols and sniffing up old blood trails. A dog could do that."

A dog has better judgment than I do. "What, am I going to be the first blood-based superhero? Here's O Positive, ready to splatter poor mooks into red paste. You're welcome, kids! I'm here all week."

"What are you, twelve?" He sounds offended, which is perhaps the most hilarious thing I've managed to accomplish in my three decades on this earth. "You could have a legacy. Change the face of this whole city."

"By bleeding on people?"

"By killing the ones who deserve it!" Leech booms in my head like a Pentecostal preacher, searing and righteous. "Start with the police. Let a single bubble of air into their bloodstreams, right at the brain stem. Problem solved."

He's got big dreams, but television doesn't tell you everything about this city. Not when they bury the truth so deep. "Yeah, yeah. Until they drop the entire department on me, and we get thrown in a Chicago-style black site. A nice personal tour of Homan Square, where the light never breaks in."

"Stop thinking so small." Leech snaps. "You can kill them too. How many police does this city have?"

A legion, swallowing two billion dollars a year so they can kick the shit out of anyone darker than a paper bag, and anyone else who dares to intervene. "Over twelve thousand."

"Easy." His anger bleeds away, leaving behind glittering malice. "We could make every single one of them pay."

I raise a brow. "And what do you get out of it?"

"Plenty to eat. I'll hollow those pigs from the inside out."

"Then who? When they're gone."

His brief spate of silence implies that I've just asked the most idiotic possible question.

"Whoever you don't like. Play superhero, Cameron. Get the cops, the corrupt politicians. The rapists. The murderers."

Hook, line, and sinker. "You're a murderer, you piece of shit parasite."

Sure, I'd slaughter the cops if it would change anything. Except the carceral fucking mentality that built them wouldn't budge an inch without people realizing why they want cops in the first place. We have to dig up the entire rotten foundation, or ten thousand new violent rubes will step into the last generation's empty boots.

Killing can even the score; peace is a different kind of work.

"My hunger is your hunger. It's what all of you want." Leech says, voice building to a violent crescendo. "More food! More sex! More drugs! More money! More *power*. Only thing that matters is bigger and better. You broadcast the same damn fantasy to each other, every waking moment."

"You've been watching too much primetime, Leech."

"Bullshit. It's a fruit growing in every skull, waiting to be plucked. Scott hated that Patricia's accident put her off fucking him. That their jobs couldn't keep food on the table. She hated him for getting a degree he didn't even use, sinking them in debt. They started hungry, but they were starving beasts by the time I was done. One chemical push does the trick. Love doesn't matter when your stomach's empty. At the end of the day, even the woman you'd give anything for is just meat."

He's trying to rile me. I can't let him. "What was the nurse's name, Leech?"

"Yvonne," he coughs out. "Happy?"

No real idea what that's like. "Sure."

"It would be easier if some faceless corporation made me in a lab and set me loose to kill the undesirables, wouldn't it? Nice people wouldn't let me just *happen* in front of them, right?" Leech giggles. "They wouldn't dance on other people's bones. They wouldn't smile in the middle of a long, slow slaughter."

But we would. We have. The blood spilled to make this place is even older than the poison infesting it now.

"Oh, I see. I was aiming for the clouds, wasn't I, Cameron?" Leech laughs, the threads of it vibrating through my throat. "You don't want to be famous. You don't want to be special. You just want to get high."

For a second, I taste my stomach lining, a vitriolic truth.

"Where's the slick comeback now, superfreak?" His taunt is cloying, sickly sweet. "You didn't do the math right, did you? If I force your old friend out, it doesn't own you anymore. Ride with me, and it's all you can eat and snort up that busted little nose."

I want it. I hate that I want it, that my blood was walled off instead of cured and the rest of my life is 'addict' in the present tense, because there *is* no cure. Even if I survive this, I'll be the exact same burnout as before.

Leech might see Patricia as meat, but we're all meat, carted around by electrical impulses and the notion that things could be better. If I take his deal, even if it feels like my fair share, it would be coming out of someone else's stomach.

I'm not a good person, but fuck—I have to be better than that.

"You killed poor people," I snap. "People starved into the smallest apartment on the block. Queer people with lives hanging on a politician's whim. Black people redlined to hell and back. This is the most segregated city in the United goddamn States. Eating a few cops won't change that, and it won't change you. Nothing good can come from what you are. What you've done."

Leech snorts. "How's the view from up on that Trojan horse? Looking at the top of the food chain and spitting on it. Nature made sure the hunger trickles down, down, down until everyone but the man in charge is starving. I'm going to use your blood to expose everyone's true colors. I'll infect them until my brothers and I are everywhere."

He can ramble as long as he wants. What I need is the best angle to smash my head into the bathroom wall, one that will break my neck instantly. I'm not leaving this bathroom as anything except a body. It has to be quick as possible, something that the blood can't pull me back from in time.

Before I'm convinced otherwise. Before I do the thing I'm best at and give in.

Someone knocks on my door, hard. "Cam! Are you in there?"

Nikki.

No, not now—

"In fact," Leech purrs, "I think the proof just arrived."

"Tell me you're okay," Nikki calls out. "It's been three days since anyone's seen you. I kept trying to call."

I was out for *three days*?

Shock leaves me exposed. Leech hauls us up and out of the tub in a flash, limbs scrabbling at the wall and sink for balance. He has me out of the bathroom before I can resist, sprinting toward the front door. I yank back with everything I have, and almost break an ankle skidding to a stop on hardwood.

"Open up, Cameron." A bile-drenched root forces its way out of my mouth, grabbing at my jaw and tongue. Another helps wrench them apart, too wide for me to speak. Panting and slavering, I try and rip the tendrils from my face, but Leech won't let my fingers catch.

"This is what she's going to see." His whisper is a cardboard rasp along the inside of my eye sockets. "The last thought in her dying brain is going to be *it was them the whole time.*"

Son of a bitch.

My hands hum with a surge of blood, turning the color of a third degree burn as I fight and claw, refusing to take another step toward the door. Leech tries to drag my legs forward like dead weight, but every time I bite down on the slick, rubbery mold in my mouth, he flinches. Even this cancerous creep has softer parts.

"Cam, I can hear you moving around in there." Nikki's so close. She must have her face pressed against the door, listening in. "If you relapsed, it's okay. You know I've got your back."

I wish. More than anything, I wish I was blitzed out of my mind. Nothing would be at risk except her quiet disappointment, followed by the malignant comfort of Nikki doing the utmost to piece me back together again. She's deserved better for so long. I can't hurt her. No matter what I have to do, Leech can't win this.

"Aren't you hungry, buddy?" Leech hums and forces his way out through my nose in bloody filaments. "I'll help you feel it."

My gut twists. I start choking on drool, and my head feels hollow and distant, scraped clean. Everything in the kitchen—the coffee, my sad protein bar collection, even the rot lurking in the garbage—turns sharp with promise. I can taste so much on the back of my tongue, but it's not what I want.

Fresh meat is on the other side of the door.

"There we go." Cramps seize my stomach as Leech whispers, the organ shrinking in on itself, withering. "Let's start with her eyes. You like those, right? They're soft. They'll go down easy, and you'll feel so much better."

The first lock opens with a quick jerk of my fingers.

"Cameron." Nikki sighs. "Please, say something."

Can't hurt her, can't hurt her, can't—

I lose a fingernail ripping my hand away from the second lock. Blood hitting air centers me for a split second, enough to start chewing like mad against Leech's roots. He hisses, pushing up from my gut with reinforcements, and it hurts. It hurts, and I'm fucking exhausted. I'm so tired of fighting for scraps every goddamn day.

"Ding ding ding!" Leech bellows. My skull echoes with it, brain bulging like an over-full balloon. "That's the dinner bell, Cameron! Eat up. Clean your fucking plate!"

He wrenches my fingers into place against the lock, turning until the bolt settles in its housing. Mordant boils the inside of my throat. The world is cast through glass, bloated from the wrong angle. It's hard to know if I have a stomach anymore, because everything below my esophagus is an open abyss, endless appetite dragging whatever dares close inside.

If I don't get to Nikki, I might devour myself.

Sweat drips into my busted nail, making me fumble the last lock, over and over. Click, click, loud as a trigger pulled right next to my ear. This shot's a blank, this one's a blank, working down the chambers until—

"Cameron?" Nikki whispers. "It is you, right?"

"Tear her apart!" Leech is twice as loud inside me, and his voice is music. Notes of yellow bile and brown decay, the milky white of new tumors. "Let the monster out."

No, please. I'll do anything.

Anything—

Leech needs my hands, but I don't.

"Cameron," Nikki warns, "I'm going to get someone to come and break down this door if you don't answer me."

"Don't," I choke out.

With the last fraction of control in my body, I slam my head into the wood so hard it rattles, forcing my hands into nail-biting fists against the door. Crescents split my palms open. I reverse the bleed, watching my fingers go marble-pale, marble-still. Pallor tapers up to each wrist as I drain them dry, leaving behind nothing but numb and empty flesh. Cyanosis chases ash gray with blue, screaming for oxygen. Without circulation, the limb will start to die, but I can't even begin to care.

"You stupid fucking—" Leech pushes up from under my skin, nodules bulging along my arms. Veins writhe and twitch in response, a nest of serpents trapping him in place. He can't beat the blood—I won't let him.

"Nikki, you have to leave." Tears cut down my face. When did I start crying? I thought I'd forgotten how. "I need you to leave me alone. Please, please..."

My body is a battlefield of warped and screaming flesh. In about two minutes, I'll have ruined both hands for good. But I can hear Nikki's pulse in a steady thrum, holding me in place until I feel her step back from the door.

"Okay." She sounds defeated, lost, but this is one fight I needed her to lose. "Okay, I'll come back tomorrow, Cam. Good to hear your voice."

Her shoes echo on the way down, and I've never been so glad for how damn loud the stairs are. The next time Leech pulls at me, I let him, falling to the floor in a convulsive fit. He paws at my hands so hard the other tendrils come to join the party, so I steal one deep, heavenly breath before relaxing.

The surge is like the ocean crashing against a dam half its size. Blood rushes back to my hands so fast that my heart staggers, missing a beat or three. Pins and needles would be a field day; this is a thousand fire ants biting down to the marrow, pulsing with countless points of agony. Red right hand, left hand, no man's land.

The funny thing about pain is eventually your brain shuts the whole operation down. One noise violation too many, and every receptor gets muzzled with a cease and desist. So it hurts, until it doesn't, and I'm still on the floor, staring at the wide open maw of death and laughing.

"Who's hungry now, huh?" I wheeze.

"If it's not her, it'll be somebody else." Leech slithers back into place, leaving me approximately human. "I got all the time in the world to beat you. Only need the once."

Maybe the redistribution of blood through my body kicked something loose, or my sanity is offering one last indulgence, but I have an idea.

"Hey, Leech."

"What?"

"Want to get takeout?"

TEN

Starvation scars more than the stomach.

It's a permanent state of being. Even if you eat again, and eat well, changing the *is* to *has* won't undo the damage. Your grandmother's famine, that anorexic summer you endured for a best friend's wedding, good old-fashioned American poverty—different methods, same results. That pang never quite fades, waiting for you to accidentally miss lunch or to stress past the tipping point, encoded into your goddamn genetics.

Leech is right about one thing: this kind of hunger makes you act out. Visceral need wears away at logic and reason like steel wool, until there's nothing left but the wanting. I started by stealing from the cafeteria at school, and ran easy cons until snagging my GED in tenth grade.

My favorite was jacking boxes of textbooks from CSU and selling them to students at a quarter the cover price; pure profit disguised as charity. Someone eventually reported my fake student ID, shoving me back to square one: scrabbling for change that slipped through society's pockets. Nothing's too low when you're born on one of the bottom rungs.

The first time I got high was because I needed relief. Because it was fun and felt good, but most importantly—the first hit was free. My intro dealer was even worse than Tommy, passing out product to kids so they'd grow into permanent customers. Eventually, 'free' turned into favors, into stealing, until there was nothing left to sacrifice at the altar of my next dose.

"You're the luckiest bastard in the world, you know that?" Leech pipes up.

He's been quiet on our way down to the street. It might be the near-death confidence talking, but I think our wrestling match tuckered him out. I can only fight him by degrees, but if the monkey slips off my back, maybe I'll outrun Leech for good.

"I have two weird entities duking it out over a body I don't even like that much, my best friend thinks I set the sobriety wagon on fire, and I'm about to go eat someone to save my own skin. 'Luck' has fallen out of my vocabulary."

"You should be dead," Leech counters. "Luck kept you from going Tommy's way. It let you survive my twin."

"How is that luck? My sanguine sovereign wanted a place to call home, and I killed your twin with a hot pot and some water. Not exactly apex predator material."

He makes me gag on spores for a good thirty seconds in response, but at this point, it feels like foreplay. If my plan works, pain is a secondary consideration. Leech can't survive killing me without someone to salvage him out of my throat, anyway.

"None of this is luck," I add, trying to clear the taste of necrotic mulch off my tongue. I'm never eating salad again. "People take care of each other here. Nikki helped me get an apartment. Maria got me a job. I saved Jasmine. It's not coincidence; we're paying it forward."

"And for what? This city hates your guts, Cameron Ciris. It hates everyone living under its gray old sky. It's eaten civilizations you can't even pronounce."

That might be true, but the hate isn't mutual.

It's why, despite myself, I can't help giving a damn. It's why I said yes to Nikki, why I've chased this rabbit hole through so many circles of hell: the Seventh Ditch and down to holy Ptolemaea. If I don't care about my corner of the world, no one will. If the 49th Ward is at peace, maybe everything that touches the edges can be too.

"Sucker," Leech hisses.

I round the corner onto Clark, and the homeless guys from the other day lean out of their alley to say hello. They stop short, eyes rounding with fear, and I wonder what exactly my face looks like now, after Leech rearranged me from the inside out. My first instinct is to apologize, to tell them that everything's fine, but I need every word I have left. If those get taken from me, I might as well lie down on the sidewalk and die.

"Why not them?" Leech mutters as I cross to the next block. "No one would miss guys like that. Two of 'em too. Lots to eat."

"If you make me puke, you're not getting anything," I mutter.

Of course, he doesn't care. Leech catcalls every passerby, distilling their virtues down to bite-size temptations. The scratch in my skull warns how deep he is, that only a single red curtain holds back annihilation.

"Is it worse to kill the mother first or the daughter first?" Leech bulldozes over my thoughts as I sidestep a woman holding her kid's hand, no more than five years old. "Because the kid would be fucked up for life, but imagine being that parent. Knowing you failed in every possible way. Not enough elasticity to heal without a scar."

"Don't have to be a parent for that," I say.

He laughs until bile spatters up to my tonsils.

Thankfully, there aren't many people around as I approach the white arch and black gates. We're at the tail end of visiting hours, and I can only hope the groundskeepers are busy mowing grass by the rich plots. Leech arrives at the obvious conclusion as I step through the gate and close it behind me, screech warped by equal parts mockery and revolted delight.

"Here? These people? Caskets full of rotten meat? You think I scavenge off the dead, you sick vulture? No, I need it raw and screaming. But if you want to play zombie, fine by me. I hope a cop sees you and arrests us, so I get a free buffet at the prison—"

I tune him out while working my way through the graves. He's not pulling at me yet, and the distraction is vital as I kneel down against cool grass and dark earth, bowing my head like I'm praying for forgiveness.

In a way, I am.

One hard lunge smashes the front of my head into the old headstone, a sharp and beveled corner splitting my temple on impact.

I bleed and gasp, "Katherine, possess me!"

She's usually gentle. Her kiss is soothing mist and concealing fog, enough to make me forget the world is made of tinder and everyone's carrying a match. Not today.

Today, Katherine is the bitter, skin-shattering burn of swallowing dry ice. She forces herself into my body like a dress three sizes too small, shoving everything out of the way for that last screaming inch of space.

The good news is, my head doesn't hurt so much anymore.

"Cameron." Katherine breathes through me, cold and crystalline. "It's crowded in here, darling. What the hell have you gotten yourself into?"

"Who is this bitch?" Leech snarls, yanking my mouth into a sneer.

"Can you shut him up, please?" I gasp.

Her accent thickens with warning. "You are not going to like it."

"I don't care, just—"

A subzero injection cuts me off. The kind of cold that kills on contact, flooding my skull with terminal brain freeze. It lasts a second, maybe two, but I'm curled up on the ground for a few minutes after, twitching violently as the blood in my veins heats back up again. Dying probably would have hurt less.

But it's quiet. For the first time in days, my mind is mercifully quiet.

"Shh, it's okay." One hand—mine, hers—strokes at the nape of my neck, drawing circles up into my hair. "I can't keep this kind of grip for long, so talk fast."

"This parasite is what's been killing people." Every word is glass slicing its way out, but the truth is the only weapon I have left. "He's growing bigger. Using me. We have to kill him, Kat. Please."

"He's in *you*," she protests. "God, Cam, everywhere. Look at your hands."

Every vein is oxidized, swollen with new growth. Bulging, slippery tendrils move under my flesh, thick as worms. I guess if Leech can't force his way into my blood, he's going to encapsulate the whole system instead.

"He almost made me eat Nikki," I say.

Katherine shudders. "She still in one piece?"

"Yeah." But now I have to keep it that way. "I need you to do me a favor, sweetheart. And I'm really sorry for asking."

"What kind of favor?"

Only her worst nightmare.

"These things are weak to heat. I parboiled the first one, but he was out in the open, easy to kill. So I need enough heat, enough fire, to cover me from head to toe."

"Cameron." Fear spreads through my chest, cold and corrosive as salt water. I can't help but feel it, when she's inside me. "You're asking for fire? Even if... Even if I can, something like that will kill you, and I can't—"

"I'm dead anyway," I interrupt, gentle as I can. "If I can have anything before the end, I want choose how I go out."

Crying stings. Her tears freeze when they meet air, frosting my eyelashes. "What if you don't come back? What if I lose you forever?"

A weak smile finds my lips. "You'll find someone better."

"I don't want *better*, you bastard!" Katherine snarls. "I want you."

"AND I WANT IN!" Leech howls.

A hard, pustular spike pierces through the back of my neck. It scrapes and digs, drilling past flesh, impaling bone. Leech rips past every layer he can, excavating with ravenous force. The world burns with a thousand imperfect colors, scorching my eyes each time he slams deep. Grabbing him is impossible; panic pulls my hands in different directions as Katherine and I fail to act in concert.

"Come on, gimme the prize," Leech hisses.

His spike comes down, and the answer is royal, raging red. He screams, impotent with shock, and tries again. It feels like he's stabbing through a rubber sheet, launched back by his own force without breaking through. Except the rubber sheet is my actual goddamn brain, and I have no idea how long the constant sluice of blood will be able to fend him off.

"The crematory!" I shout. "Take us, Katherine! Now!"

All I can think as we limp out of the cemetery like the living dead is that someone is going to see us. I've ignored a lot of weird shit in my day, but the barefoot guy smoking weed on the train in a GOD FORGOT US shirt at 2 a.m. is a lot easier to write off than this sloughing rat tail trying to give me a lobotomy.

Thankfully, Chicago's grid of streets hasn't changed much in the last century. As Katherine yanks me through alleys and under stairwells, Leech's incessant prodding starts to slow down. Painful as it is, splitting his focus means he can't keep playing tug-of-war with the rest of my body.

She stumbles to a stop at the intersection of Thorndale and Clark. "Where from here?"

"Two blocks over," I grit out.

Leech tears up through my guts. He can't get far without drawing blood and pissing off everything attached, but feeling organs knot and unravel is a trauma I hoped to keep off the books. If Katherine could feel pain, this would be over, but for better or worse, there's no overlap. She's unstoppable, running me like a T-1000 down the street until the front of All Paws Go to Heaven comes into view.

Katherine tries to shove the door open, but it rattles and resists.

"Check the sign," I say.

"Out for lunch?" She pushes again. "Goddamn it."

Neil, how do you manage to fuck me over without even being here?

The depraved cackle echoing from my pituitary gland—did I mention I hate this guy?—is insult to injury. "You're so weak, Cameron. Your blood's got no fight left."

"Break the glass," I say to Katherine.

I won't be around to see the consequences, anyway. She grabs the entry bar for leverage and kicks the bottom pane with as much force as we can muster. Cracks spiderweb across the point of impact; she does it again. The result is a horrifying, splintered gap I have to climb through, but my fear doesn't matter when Katherine's in the driver's seat. We emerge in the half-light of the lobby, surrounded by false eyes and an ark's worth of animals locked in a soulless parade of joy.

"Over the counter—*fuck*—"

Leech has a solid hold on the door, his tendril wrapped around in crusting coils, the slick membrane drying before my eyes. I'm not the only one who's weak.

"Left pocket, Katherine," I gasp.

She dives in, fingers fishing around to grab my lancet. The blade is tiny but surgically sharp, and even with Leech keeping a leash on my head, he can't get away without letting go. Katherine whips my wrist into a clean, graceful cut. So graceful that I'm suddenly certain she's stabbed someone to death in the past, and never bothered to mention it before.

The good part is that she shreds through half the membrane in one slice. The bad part is that it's only half, and I learn that Leech is buried deep enough in my system for me to feel the blade. I flinch, diverting Katherine's next cut, and Leech yanks at my skull so hard it shrinks my vision to pinpoints of black.

"Can't see—"

My arm moves. Something slick answers, and the tightrope of tension holding me to the door vanishes in another hot burst of pain. "Don't worry, sweet thing. My eyes work fine."

"Give it back!" Leech flails wildly, the stump attached to my head splashing fluid across my shoulders. Drops of red drip through the black, but it's thick as sap. I taste salt like someone upended a shaker in my mouth. "You can't cut out the rest of me, Cameron! Even if you burn yourself alive!"

"Won't matter when I'm ash, asshole."

My body really must be running on fumes, because Katherine has to use the door proper rather than climbing up over the counter. Past Neil's cushy chair and a mountain of paperwork is a heavy set of keys. Katherine grabs it and keeps moving, using me like a bludgeon to shove the next door to the furnace open.

The room is pitch black, desert-hot. Leech hisses like an egg frying on the sidewalk, and his instinctive recoil proves this is the right decision. A huge steel valve bars the way, but Katherine turns it with well-oiled ease. The interior glares orange with old heat, enough to give me a sunburn, but nowhere what I need.

Next to the mouth of the furnace is a box with more buttons and knobs than I can count, each one a different color and patterned with symbols. With only a faint glow for light, I can't read the text underneath.

"Tell me what everything says, Katherine," I say.

"Ah, master cycle. Throat air. Ignition burner delay?" Fear tightens her words. Even if she can't feel through my skin, the waiting blaze is right in Katherine's face. "I don't know what a damn one of these do."

"You're not going to kill yourself," Leech snaps, tone swinging wild between rage and command. "Even if you are a selfish piece of shit. The second you feel that fire, you'll be begging for my help. She will be too. Your hanger-on is sweating more than I am."

"Shut up!" I snap. "Turn the delay to zero. What else?"

"Pollution alarm. Burner reset. Power on."

"Turn the alarm off. Then push the next ones in order." Neil does this every day, so it can't be too complicated. "I'm sorry, Kat. I love you. That will always be true."

Her answering wail wrenches my voice to a higher pitch than it's been in years, but she mashes my fingers against the buttons. The sliver of orange in my vision brightens, caught like a piece of the sun.

"I love you too," Katherine whispers.

"Think of everything you're giving up!" Leech screams. "You want forever? I'll give you forever! The world is your open fucking oyster, Cameron! Just eat it! *Eat it*."

Choke on me, motherfucker.

"Kat, pull the door shut once I'm in."

My clothes catch first, cotton igniting on contact. There's no next breath when the first one chars my lungs from the inside out. Steel clangs, fingers peeling down to sizzling fat. Adrenaline devours pain until the fuse of every nerve is exposed.

Leech screams, and I smile with blackened teeth.

ELEVEN

I'M IN THE HOSPITAL for two weeks, which is a lot longer than they keep most corpses around.

The nurses loved that joke in the burn ward. I turned up charred to a crisp, assigned DOA until the tech about to shove me in the morgue did a mandated pulse check. I scared him half to death before he summoned every doctor in earshot. They threw me a party like I hadn't seen in months, flashing surgical lights and dancing IVs, paring away a charcoal layer of hard, dead flesh until finding my body underneath, fresh as a butterfly from the cocoon.

Being a 'medical miracle' lost its shine after the police took witness testimony from Neil, who had the mixed fortune of finding my half-torched cremains. He also had an alibi for not being in the shop, which pinned my personal conflagration as attempted suicide. The cops threatened to arrest me over forcible entry until a psych at the hospital took me under her wing. Paying for the busted door and more piss tests than I could count set me back a chunk of change, but without evidence of illegal intoxication in my system, her official report wrote me off as a pathetic loser on the edge.

My job is the only reason I didn't walk out half a million in debt. Insurance covers a lot of sins when you work in the healthcare sector, even as a janitor. Writing the rest of my case off as charity made the hospital look good, a quick ego stroke over not accidentally throwing me in the freezer. Far as I can tell, I would have woken up by myself at some point, but doing it in an icebox while clawing out of a casket of my own scorched skin is less than ideal.

Katherine stayed in the furnace as long as she could, until the sun dragged her back to the cemetery. I visit her every night before work now, partially to apologize and partially so she can slip inside and make sure no new visitors are using my gut flora for a midnight snack. Asking your girlfriend to kill you leaves a lot of baggage at the front door, especially when it forced her to face the same thing she died from.

I don't know how to fix that yet, but I'm trying.

Nikki took the news worse than anyone. She blames herself for not forcing her way into the apartment that night, and I can't offer up the truth as salvation. Promising there's nothing she could have done doesn't work when the illusion of opportunity was right in front of her. I fed her the same lie as the psych—that it wasn't a planned suicide attempt but a sudden urge, brought on by so many people dying around me. Never mind that I wasn't trying to kill myself to begin with. My life was the price of wiping out Leech, not the upside.

Whatever. He's dead and I'm not.

I'm tugging on my new jacket from Xanthous when there's a knock at the door. Nikki, right on schedule. Opening the locks still makes my shoulders tense up around my ears, but she's the only one waiting on the other side.

"Hey, Cam." Her smile rises easier than it has in weeks. "Ready for brunch?"

"You bet. Lead the way."

This is part of our new routine—eating at the diner by the north end of Clark on Saturdays. It lets her keep an eye on me, and it lets me enjoy time with a friend that has nothing to do with blood or wayward bodies.

Lexi's is a holdover from the 60s, with speckled laminate countertops and puce seat cushions that have been perpetually sewn back into working order. The host tells us to take a booth anywhere like Nikki and I don't always grab the same one in the very back. Our waitress doesn't bother with menus, merely leaning out of the kitchen to meet my eyes.

"The usual?" she asks.

I answer at the same time as Nikki, producing a hybrid between "yes" and "please" that sounds like the title of a concept album.

Our mutual gargle earns a grin, and the waitress vanishes back into the kitchen without another word.

Nikki picks out a pair of sugar packets to prep for her soon-to-arrive coffee. "Has work started giving you full shifts yet?"

"Yeah. I'm forbidden from overtime for another six months, though. They don't want to get sued for stressing me out."

"Well, can't blame them for that." Her smile is tight with sympathy. Guilt does a two-step across my stomach. "You were working two jobs at once."

"I like *both* of my jobs," I protest. "It doesn't feel right to give up helping the neighborhood because my brain tripped and fell on its self-destruct mechanism."

She opens her mouth—probably to remind me not to be so bleak—when our food arrives in a jostling clink of plates and cups. Nikki gets blonde roast, orange juice, and their weekend French toast special stacked up half a foot high. Mine is two steaks rare enough to bleed, overlapping a pair of runny eggs and one narrow triangle of bread.

"You should ask them to bring the cow to the table and cut it in half," Nikki jokes. "It would save you some time."

I force a smile, tasting cinders. "Would if I could."

For days, I threw up everything they gave me in the hospital, until some enterprising physician ran tests and discovered my body was on the nigh-lethal end of protein and iron deficiency. They fed me enough stewed chicken and rice to make an Olympian athlete choke until the nausea passed.

The rice made me sick too, but that was easier to hide. My attending blamed it on autophagy, declaring my body had eaten into its own muscle tissue to force so much healing so fast. I was just glad they already had a word on the books. Having a definition brought the hospital comfort, enough to keep from digging too deep.

Meat is the only thing I can stomach. Eggs are neutral territory if they're close to raw, but offal goes down the easiest. Even the bread on my plate is only for show, something to nibble at if it's soaked in drippings, enough fat to disguise the source on the way in. So I cut my steaks into careful pieces like I don't want to jam the whole mass into my mouth, I laugh at Nikki's jokes, and sometimes, I can pretend everything is like it used to be.

Temptation has my number on speed dial. The blood keeps calling to me, and so does Leech, in his own way. I remember Terrance and Yvonne, the Hayes's, the Norths, and everyone else he tore apart like the kills were my own. Nothing else tastes like they did, but I can treat the symptoms even if there's no cure.

If I never go hungry again, the urge can't take over. I promised myself that.

Cross my heart, and hope to die.

Acknowledgments

First and foremost, I'd like to thank Eric Raglin, who I not only had the pleasure of working with for the anthology *Shredded* but who also gave the feedback that finally molded this book into its proper grotesque shape. Thank you also to Kat, Ave, and Liv, who walked and talked around the neighborhood with me many a time when the words needed more encouragement to flow. And to any fans of my romance work - I absolutely appreciate you taking a chance on a completely different genre from me.

About the Author

Rien Gray is a disabled agender butch from Chicago with ten published novellas focused on trans and sapphic romance, eroticism, fantasy, and horror. They have one completed series beginning with *Love Kills Twice*, and another ongoing series beginning with *Valerin the Fair*. When not writing, they're probably lifting weights or chasing a platinum trophy in a video game.